Event Survivors
By: Ron Mueller

Books by Ron Mueller

The Alex Evercrest Series-Detective
  The River Front
  The Girl on the Grill
  Missing
  Maggot
  Racist
  Votive Candles
  Windy City
  Country Road
  Pool of Blood
  Sins of the Daughter

The Door Series-Science Fiction
  The Door

The Savitar Series-Science Fiction
  Journey's End
  Savitar
  Confluence

Bram Nielson Series-Science Fiction
  The Fold
  The Message
  Fold Wormhole
  Negative Fold
  Ripples in Time

The Taelo Series-Prehistory America
  Taelo: The Early Years
  Taelo: The Golden Feather
  Taelo: Journey of Discovery
  Taelo: Dangerous Passage
  Taelo: Condor Clan Slingers
  Taelo: Circumvention
  Taelo: The Journey of Sages

A Taelo Story
  The Name of the Child
  White Swan and Quiet Pheasant
  Broken Spear
  Floating Cloud
  Quiet Rabbit
  Busy Bee
  Little Otter& Talking Wren
  Burley Bear & Meadow Flower

A Feather-in-the-Wind Story
  The Eastern Elk Clan

  The Problem Solver Series-Secret Agent
  The Beginning
  Drug Lords
  Broder Crosser

  Current Past and Future-Science Fiction
  Event Survivors-Science Fiction
  The Door-Science Fiction
  Viajante 7-Science fiction
  Imagination by Courtney Huynh and Chloe Parker

Event Survivors
By: Ron Mueller

Around the World Publishing LLC
4914 Cooper Road Suite 144
Cincinnati, Ohio 45242-9998

Event Survivors by Ron Mueller Copyright © 2012.
© 2023

ISBN 13: 978-1-68223-319-1
ISBN 10: 1-68223-319-7

Distributed by Ingram
Cover Picture By: Yiannos1, Dreamstime.com
Cover Design By: Ron Mueller

Ron Mueller

Table of Content

Introduction to Event Survivors — 1
Chapter 1: Buchanan, Virginia — 3
Chapter 2: New Year — 15
Chapter 3: Anna, Sao Paulo — 27
Chapter 4: Muri and John, Africa — 49
Chapter 5: Cualli and Tosi, Mexico — 57
Chapter 6: Lucas, Buchanan, Virginia — 65
Chapter 7: The Party — 77
Chapter 8: Anna — 89
Chapter 9: Muri — 97
Chapter10: Cualli and Tosi — 103
Chapter 11: Clair — 111
Chapter 12: Up the Trail — 117
Chapter 13: Anna, on the Trail — 127
Chapter 14: Muri, John, and tortoise — 135
Chapter 15: Cualli, Tosi and Dolphins — 143
Chapter 16: Clair, Anna, Lady, and the Tramp — 149
Chapter 17: Homestead and winter — 155
Chapter 18: Sunlight — 165
Chapter 19: Muri, John, the Journey — 173
Chapter 20: Cualli, Tosi, the Lucky Lady — 189
Chapter 21: New Home — 197
Chapter 22: The Garden — 209
Chapter 23: Contact — 223
Chapter 24: Homestead — 239
Chapter 25: Muri, John traveling Africa — 255
Chapter 26: Cualli, Tosi, Sailing East — 267
Chapter 27: Recovery and the Norfolk — 277
Chapter 28: West to East, North to South — 287
Chapter 29: Cualli, Tosi, Australia — 297
Chapter 30: Epilogue — 307
About the Author — 313
Characters in the Story

<u>Introduction</u>

The present time period is experiencing a ten times faster than normal change in the position of the Earth's North pole leads to the speculation that this is leading up to the Event predicted by the Aztecs.
Aztec mythology is full of wrath, death, and enough cataclysmic destruction to make the end of the world seem tame. The Aztecs regularly discussed the end of the world and sacrificed people to prevent it.

The *Stone of the Sun*, an Aztec artifact, predicts a world changing event that is to happen during our current epoch. Prehistoric evidence indicates that something similar may have occurred in Earth's distant past. Speculation by some scientists say it is happening as I write this book.

The *Stone of the Sun* is not a calendar. It's really the image of space and time. It's an image of how the Aztecs conceived themselves as in the center of time and space. *[1]

The gods of the Aztec cosmos favor the human heart, which is torn from the living body as an offering. Appeasing these gods reaches a fifty thousand per year crescendo. Reports of the blood-drenched ceremonies strike terror into the Aztec enemy hearts required for sacrifice.

There are two calendars. One covering 365 days and one 260 days.

Every day has multiple shadings of possible meaning. It is a richly rewarding way to go through time. Each day is percolating with different meanings and recollections and hopes.

It's not about the world ending; it's about cycles of time and the changes that happen in each cycle.

The concepts and stories told by the Aztec are mild compared to the devastation, turmoil, and pain that those who perished and those who survived would experience and endure during the EVENT.

Each region of the world would have a different experience and survivors would respond differently.

Would there be any survivors in the scenario depicted in this book?

Would they have the ability to recover?

Would good triumph?

1* by Diana Megaloni Kerpel Mexico City Museum Director

Chapter 1: Buchanan, Virginia

Lucas sat on what had been his father's dark pine green Adirondack chair looking out into the Virginia valley to where Buchanan was sitting on the bank of the James River. He of course could not see beyond the end of his snow-covered drive. He was sitting out on the wide veranda in the December cold feeling sorry for himself.

Two year ago, Lucas had moved back home when his sixty-three-year-old father died of what Lucas thought of as miner's lung disease that his father had gotten when working in the coal mines. He did not want to leave his mother alone and decided to move back to where he had grown up.

To return home he had left a very lucrative architectural position in Boston and had taken an offer from a small Buchanan firm owned by one of his father's old friends.

Lucas was an only child born just after his mother turned forty. This was late in life for a child, and he was the only one. He and his mother were close.

Soon after his father's death, he watched as she seemed to deteriorate before his eyes. Her doctors could find no reason for her decline.

Lucas had grown up in the warm shadow of the love between his father and his mother. He figured she missed him so much that she died of a broken heart. There was no other explanation.

She seemed to know her time. She said good night to him and reminded him of how proud she was of him and how much she loved him. Lucas took note that it was almost to a day of her June wedding anniversary and the family garden was in full bloom. His mother died in her sleep.

He cried for a week. It seemed twice as impactful as when his father had passed away.

He supposed his Dad would have been jealous of how he mourned his Mom. But maybe not because he too loved her so much. Lucas missed them both intensely. Losing both of them in just two years overwhelmed him.

The two events had been devastating. There were no other close family members. Their three-person unit had been the foundation of his being. Their family garden had been their bonding site.

The garden and part time jobs had been how his Dad had supported the three of them. It was in the garden that Lucas had learned about how to deal with life.

The garden had got all his attention and spare time through the summer after his Mother's passing. The harvest in the fall was one of the best he had ever experienced.

It just made him cry harder.

He reflected on the help his few close friends had extended to him as they tried to console him. He really appreciated their efforts.

The current grey, cold, erratic weather was to him a stark reflection of what he looked at in the mirror each morning. He realized he was looking more like an old man than someone in his thirties.

Lucas, empty coffee cup in hand stood up and looked down the deep snow-covered driveway leading down to the main road. Even if he cleared his driveway, the main road would not be cleared. There was no way to drive over to his neighbors for the Christmas dinner to which he was invited.

He went into the house and prepared to snowshoe across the ridge to their home. They had moved in during the summer and he had become a frequent visitor. Their five-year old daughter Clair and how warmly she always greeted her "Uncle" Lucas was the key reason he had been looking forward to Christmas. He was glad that he had shopped early for the doll Clair had said she wanted.

Lucas had done his Christmas shopping right after Thanksgiving. At the time he thought he had paid too much for the doll but now that the weather had closed in, he was happy that he bought it when he did.

Lucas prepared himself and his gear to make the mile hike along the mountain ridge. He would face blowing wind deep snow for the entire way. He would be snowshoeing the entire way. He figured it would be almost a day long hike in the three feet of snow that covered the ground.

Lucas hiked through the garden to the trail head at the far corner. The wind had picked up and he knew he would be challenged by the deteriorating weather.

Lucas knew he looked like one of those arctic explorers shown on the National Geographic pictures. He had on a full pull over head covering, ski goggles, a hooded fleece jacket, ski gloves, and thermal pants. Even his toes, covered by two thick socks and protected by his leather hiking boots, were warm. He had been taught well and had hiked in the winter many times.

Lucas set a steady pace along the ridge. The fresh three-foot-high snow and the occasionally snow drifts blocking his way provided more of a challenge than he had imagined. Just as he was beginning to worry, he spotted the smoke spiraling out of the chimney of Jim and Evelyn's large, old log home.

The invite had been for a six pm dinner. He had not been able to contact the two. The mountain was a cell phone dead spot and the landline had gone down over night.

Lucas was looking forward to dinner.

Lucas took off his wool face mask and goggles before knocking on the door. Evelyn opened the door and let out a gasp of surprise.

Lucas could hear the crackling and see the fire in the living room. Jim stood up and held up a beer and pointed to it. Warm air greeted his face.

It was the squeal of delight from Clair that brought instant warmth to his entire body.

He stepped into the entry area and took off all of his outer clothing. Then he gave Clair a hug. He turned down the beer and asked if he could have a cup of hot tea.

Lucas's breath stopped when a stunning younger version of Evelyn stepped out of the kitchen. Her long blond hair, crystal clear blue eyes, a twinkle in her eyes and a radiant smile held his full attention.

He finally saw the mug in her hand as she repeated the word tea as she held it out to him.

Involuntarily Lucas looked over at the picture of Amanda on the fireplace. The young girl in the picture had turned into a knee weakening devastating beauty.

Evelyn gave him an elbow in the ribs and told Lucas to close his mouth and behave as she introduced Amanda.

Lucas shook Amanda's hand and felt an instant electricity. It was hard not to stare. Her eyes seemed to capture his.

Lucas listened to Amanda as she explained that she had brought a supply of Jasmine tea because she knew Evelyn was a coffee hound and she would only have old bags of Lipton tea left over from making iced tea in the summer.

Lucas nodded and continued to stare into her eyes and concentrated on not drooling. He would have to talk to Evelyn about putting up a more recent picture of her sister on the fireplace mantel.

Clair helped Lucas get refocused. He walked over to his backpack and put his three presents under the Christmas tree. Clair was immediately checking her present out.

Lucas teased Clair about what it might be, and she would never guess what it was.

He was sure that the dinner that followed was very good. The only thing he could remember about it was trying not to stare at Amanda, who was sitting directly across from him.

There was no television. Lucas had satellite reception at his place, but Jim and Evelyn had a less expensive plan using their phone and internet connection. It was all down.

They sat around chatting until it was time to go to sleep. Clair was asleep by nine. The rest of them stayed up talking about work, neighbors and what Amanda was planning to do when she graduated from Virginia Tech.

Lucas got his sleeping bag and rolled it out in front of the fireplace. He was glad that he had brought his flannel pajamas. He usually slept in the nude. The lights went out and he lay on his sleeping bag enjoying the remainder of the fire.

The dying fire was down to a few red coals and Lucas was almost asleep when he felt a soft touch on his shoulder. A shiver went from head to foot as he heard Amanda whisper and ask if he would mind if she joined him.

Lucas closed his eyes and took in the sweet fragrance of her skin as he felt the touch of her hand on his cheek.

He rolled toward her, and she leaned in for a kiss. The ashes in the fireplace were cold and dawn was arriving when Amanda retreated back to her bedroom, Lucas felt like the Cheshire cat. He knew he would have a hard time not fawning over her during the day.

A few moments later he watched as Clair came quietly into the great room and sat looking at the presents under the Christmas tree. Lucas stood up gave Clair a hug and then went into the guest bathroom for a quick shower before everyone else got up.

Lucas was sitting with a cup of coffee reading a story to Clair when Evelyn came in and gave Clair and him a hug and wished them both a good morning. She asked if he had a good night's sleep and asked if anyone wanted some bacon and eggs for breakfast.

He was not going to complain about a lack of sleep. Instead, he ate a hearty breakfast and joined Jim in the family room where the fire was once again at a full blaze.

Amanda finally joined the rest of the family when it was time to open the presents. Lucas could not believe she could look so fresh and alluring.

He knew he was tired and low on energy and probably looked just like he felt.

Clair was the center of attention. Evelyn handed her one present at a time and made sure to take a picture of her opening it before giving her the next one. Every present got a squeal of pleasure and then got quickly put aside so the next one could be opened. The last gift was the one Lucas had brought. It was the only doll that Clair had received. That was not an accident, and it was not about Lucas being a great gift selector. Evelyn had told him exactly what doll Clair wanted. She had told him what store had the best price and she had had let him know what accessories would also be appreciated.

Lucas had done the man thing. He had bought the doll, wrapped it, and brought it over at the right time. He was happy to have had the guidance and he was now enjoying the way Clair was reacting to the doll.

Evelyn whispered her thanks for getting the doll over in time for Christmas. Lucas smiled and replied he would not have missed it.

He looked over to Amanda and gave her smile.

After the gift opening and a light lunch, Lucas began to get ready to hike home. It was starting to snow again. He thought about leaving his gear but decided that it was his insurance if he got caught in the storm and failed to get home.

Amanda asked if she could join him for the hike back to his place. Nothing would have made him happier, but he gave a no in reply.

Amanda made a sly comment about the fact that she was in good shape and took a ski pose.

He would have loved to have her come with him and spend time in front of the fireplace in his family room, but it was just too dangerous.

He asked her if she had ever hiked a mile in snowshoes with wind trying to sweep her off the trail.

Evelyn saved the day by asking if Lucas could open up the road and come by the following day.

Lucas promised to give it a try and put the sandwich Evelyn offered into his backpack.

Seeing Amanda again was all the incentive Lucas needed.

Evalyn told him that Amanda was staying until the New Year.

He thanked her for the great Christmas Eve dinner and opened the door and took in the heavy snow that was coming down. It would be impossible for him to navigate the trail.

He turned and asked whether he could stay for another cup of tea and closed the door behind him.

That night was a repeat of the night before and it had a huge emotional impact on him.

Another two feet of snow came down during the day. He knew that the next morning he would need to return. He had chickens and rabbits that needed attention.

He left early in the morning and found the hike to be a challenge as he slowly worked his way through the snow-covered trail. Fortunately, the ridge was mostly open, and the wind had kept the snow level low enough for him to work his way through.

The warming lights and the self-feeders had done their job. Everything at his place was in order. He filled the feeders and proceeded to the house.

Lucas brought the temperature of the house back up to a comfortable level. He checked out the plow mounted on the front of his pick-up truck. He put five one-hundred-pound feed bags in the bed of the pickup and then began the job of clearing his lane.

It took him two days to open a single lane from is place to Jim and Evelyn's place. He enjoyed lunch with the Egalston's and then went to work clearing a path down to the main road. He knew that the road up the mountain would be last on the counties work list.

The next day, Lucas was surprised by a knock on the door and more surprised when he opened it to find Amanda.

Amanda boldly announce that she had come over to chase him around naked and then planted a kiss that threatened to cause him to faint.

Lucas lifted her up, closed the door with his foot and carried her to the front of the fireplace. Why don't you join me in the shower and afterwards you can do the chasing Lucas suggested?

He felt renewed. He thought of the love between his parents and wondered if he might have found someone with whom he could have the same relationship.

It was New Year's Eve day. Amanda and Lucas spent the day frolicking and enjoying each other. Then they enjoyed another mutual shower and left to go to Evelyn's and Jim's New Year's Eve party.

Lucas claimed innocents when Evelyn asked about his intentions with Amanda. He knew he was smitten by Amanda but not sure what her feelings toward him might be.

14

<u>Chapter 2: New Year</u>

ℒucas experienced an emotional slide down from the New Year to into early spring. The winter continued dumping snow and then cycling into the higher melting temperatures and then back to more snow. While searching the internet about developing his writing skills Lucas began to see a pattern of natural disasters. Not really a pattern but a tone of being erratic, more violent, and extreme and destructive. The articles always came back to the topic of global warming.

Lucas thought that was the case too, but he also wondered if the global warming might be caused by something other than or in addition to some other phenomenon that might be occurring.

He noted that the true North Pole was currently at an extreme swing just north of the Russian coast. Also, the number locations and power of Earthquakes was hitting a record high. And finally, the pattern of storms and the amounts of rain and snow were happening in unexpected locations.

Lucas saw no pattern but a lot of extreme activity.

Lucas had his hopes of seeing Amanda during her spring break dashed when she invited him to go on spring break with her to Florida.

He politely said no and invited her to stop by on her way back if she could. Lucas immediately called himself a series of derogatory names. Stupid was his least offensive deprecation. He should have taken her offer, but he found it hard to picture letting himself frolic like all the crazy young people did during spring break.

Lucas's exciting spring activities were to till the garden and to order one hundred chicks. Both the garden and the raising of the chickens for himself and to sell were part of the family practice that he was still carrying on.

By the end of June, the garden would be in full bloom and the chickens would soon be butchered, wrapped, and froze.

This year he would share the garden and his chickens with Evelyn, Jim, and Clair. Lucas planned to give the folks in his office a share as well. He certainly would not be able to consume all that he was growing.

Chickens, rabbits, and garden instead of Amanda. He was certain that is qualified him as being stupid.

Lucas looked at the adorable baby rabbits. Some were black and white. Another group were a light cream color. His favorite family were all black. He kept each type of rabbit in separate pens. This kept them from cross breeding.

Each group was made up of two does and one buck. Each group produced close to one hundred eighty pounds of meat per year.

Lucas had four family groups and produced close to seven hundred pounds of rabbit meat per year. He sold the meat at eight dollars a pound. Each of his rabbit families netted about a thousand dollars per year.

As much as he loved to handle the young rabbits, Lucas made sure not to get attached to any of the young. They were cute but they were the crop to be harvested.

His attachment was to the does and bucks. He retired them and let them expire due to old age when they got too old to produce.

The garden was another attachment that pulled on Lucas. He carefully put in the seeds that could stand the temperature swings. The other plants were started in starter flats and kept in the shed at about sixty degrees under multi-frequency lights. They got planted once the risk of frost diminished.

Lucas went by the Farmer's Almanac. He also trended the weather and listened to the local farm station. His most valuable resources were the old farmers with whom he had breakfast down in Buchanan. It was a game of getting the timing right. Plant too early and you lose the delicate plants. Plant too late and the harvest is less than expected.

Lucas managed to overcome the reality of Amanda's silence by keeping busy around the homestead. He was self-conscious of the ten-year age difference between them.

He was sure she would move on to some younger, more upscale suitor.

A strange blue Mustang was parked in his driveway as he returned from work. Lucas parked his truck and began to look around for the driver of the car.

Amanda and another good-looking young lady, each holding a young rabbit came walking out of what Lucas called his rabbit barn. Blonde, blue eyed, Amanda had selected one of the pure black rabbits and her black haired, dark brown eyed friend had an almost blond Champagne D Argent rabbit.

Lucas looked at the ying and yang of the two young women.

Lucas's surprise was followed by a surge of warmth. He could not help but feel a rush of desire.

He wanted to rush forward and plant a big kiss on Amanda but instead shook Rachel's hand when Amanda made the introduction.

"Can we keep these rabbits?" Was a question that surprised Lucas.

"Yes, take them to Evelyn. She asked for a couple," was his reply.

Will you take us hiking? Was the next question.

Sure, when would you like to hike?

They agreed to the Saturday.

Rachel inquired about what to wear.

Jeans, a warm shirt, and a light jacket was his reply.

Lucas volunteered to bring a picnic lunch.

He then extended the hike into an invitation for a night out on the town.

"Buchanan is a hopping town on a Friday night," he joked.

His goal was to maximize his time with Amanda.

Night life in Buchanan, really! Amanda said in a snarky, snide remark made as she gave him a radiant smile.

"Yes, with dinner, a movie and a stop to Brian's pub and you experience eighty five percent of what is available.

Then we can choose from a high school play, perhaps a school baseball game or bingo at the Baptist church.

On the other hand, we can save most of this for when you need excitement on another day," Lucas rattled off and gave his own broad smile in return.

Do you have a friend that can join us for this exciting night out or is it just us? Rachel asked.

"Yes, I have a couple in mind. Let me call and ask," Lucas replied.

"Do you have a specific kind of guy that would be of interest to you," he inquired?

"Yes, I like ones that can carry on a conversation about something other than sports, or how much they can drink," was Rachel's reply.

He knew of a dozen that would line up to go out with either of the two young beauties standing before him. Her specification cut that down to about three people, and two of them were married.

He knew that after their spring break activities the activities around Buchanan might seem rather tame and backwoods. He would enjoy them greatly if he was spending his time with Amanda.

"Well, let's get up to Evelyn's, she is expecting us for dinner. What time tomorrow should we plan for our Buchanan night life tour," Amanda asked as she got in the car and situated her rabbit in her lap?

"What should I call my rabbit," she asked through the window?

"Oh, I wouldn't give it a name just yet," Lucas replied.

But he knew immediately that he would need to bring some other rabbits up to Evelyn. These two would enjoy a long life and have names. He hoped they would make good breeder bucks or does.

Lucas watched the Mustang turn and go up toward Evelyn's homestead.

Lucas immediately put in a call to his friend Jeff. Jeff was the junior editor of the Buchanan Express. He was a fun guy to be around. He would often skip the drinking to listen to the discussions of those drinking. These became the kernel of the editorial stories that he wrote. His writing skills had single handedly increased the circulation of the paper. Lucas was one of his new subscribers.

Jeff's reply was somewhat cynical. "Don't tell me she has a good personality" was all he said.

Lucas countered with the fact that she was simply gorgeous, and that Jeff would have to be the judge of her personality.

"Trust me heads will turn when we walk in with these two beauties on our arms. People will be buying the Express just to see if you write something about these two," Lucas replied.

Lucas and Jeff agreed to the River Inn for dinner and the Buchanan Theatre for their current show and a walk across the James River on the hanging bridge

Neither of them knew what was showing at the theater so it would be a surprise.

Finally, they would go to the Chopper Top for a night cap. There was not much else to do. They would have to branch out to other cities if there would ever be a second date.

Lucas hung up the phone and went about watering and feeding the chickens and the rabbits.

He then went to the garden. This was his magical part of the homestead. A small natural spring gurgled up out of the ground on the high-end back end of the garden. It provided a continuous source for a continuous irrigation system. The garden always had plenty of water and was a prolific provider of vegetables. Lucas continued to plant the garden at its full capacity.

He had made arrangements with the churches in the community to distribute his garden vegetables to their needy members.

He made it a point to walk the garden on a daily basis. This was the place he remembered both his father and mother. He talked to them on a daily basis.

Lucas was just coming out of the shower thinking about his current pattern of living when he was startled by noise in the kitchen.

Alarm bells went off as he grabbed the bat he kept in the bedroom. He crept quietly across the great room toward the kitchen.

Amanda walked through the doorway with two cups of tea in hand.

"You look great in your briefs. Not bad for an old man. How about some tea," Amanda said with a bright smile?

What are you doing here? Lucas asked as he took the tea.

"Well, Evelyn wanted me to tell you the rabbits you sent with Rachel, and I got names. You need to bring some for the grill.

Evelyn sent some broiled chicken, green beans, and potatoes for your dinner, so I brought that over too," Amanda said as she went to the couch and sat down.

I decided to deliver the message myself and see if I could seduce you.

Lucas was glad she had given a long explanation. He was trying to get his emotions under control. He hustled back to the bedroom to put on some clothes before he embarrassed himself.

Amanda was dressed to seduce, and she was having the desired effect on him. She was in short shorts and a tight V necked top and looked delicious.

He hoped she was dessert.

"You look great. Thanks for bringing dinner over. I usually just reheat something I cooked on the weekend," Lucas said as he took his cup of tea and sat down next to Amanda.

"Well, after you eat, take me for a walk around the homestead," Amanda said as she got up, took his hand, and led him into the kitchen.

"Evelyn says everything in this dinner is from your place, the chicken, the potatoes, the salad, and the tomatoes. She said to thank you for the generous supply of all the food. She wanted you to know the money being saved on food is going into Clair's college fund. This is the first time they have been able to get ahead," Amanda said as she guided Lucas into the kitchen.

It's good that she is thinking ahead to Clair's college. It makes me feel good that I can contribute to Clair's college fund.

The chicken was delicious. Lucas could tell it was the recipe his mom had left him, and he had given to Evelyn after eating her first try at baked chicken. That chicken had been dry and almost tasteless. Tonight, Lucas knew Evelyn had mastered his mother's simple recipe.

Lucas was still wondering about desert as he rinsed his dishes and put them into the dishwasher.

The tour of the homestead provided him time to listen to Amanda's questions and to try to get past her allure. He showed her the garden and then took her farther along the trail and showed her the cave.

The cave still had the fort and sleeping area he had used when he was young. He maintained an emergency supply of food, some clothes and a first aid kit. He also had an old rocking chair and stool. This was where he went to be secluded and alone. During his high school years, it had been the place to hide for the night if he had been drinking.

"This cave has been my private space all my life. Mom and Dad knew if I said I was going to the cave it meant I wanted to be alone. I loved to come here and sit and read. Sometimes I came here to do my homework. I slept off every high school party here in my fort," Lucas said as Amanda settled on his lap.

After a few deep kisses, it was Amanda who led the way out of the cave back towards the house.

"I can't believe you raise these cute bunnies for food. Evelyn says your mother's roast rabbit recipe is out of this world. I'll try it and it better be good. I want you to promise me that my rabbit will not become a roast," Amanda said as she was about to pick up another one of the young rabbits.

"Why don't you just pet one of the grown rabbits? They have names and they will live to ripe old ages," Lucas suggested and brought out one of the mother rabbits. "Your rabbit will become one of them."

"Is your rabbit male or female," Lucas asked?

"I don't know. I didn't think to look," Amanda replied as she looked at and reached out for one of the mother rabbits.

"Wow she is big. I didn't know they got this big," Amanda said as she scratched one of the mother rabbits behind the ear.

Lucas led the way back to the house and gave Amanda the tour of the house. She was surprised at the cool room built into the rock of the mountain. It was the place where Lucas kept all the fresh vegetables and canned goods. There was a freezer that held the butchered meat. The cool room was also where he kept an ample supply of wine. He had a small but varied collection. He took a Muscat he had picked up in Italy and led the way back to the kitchen.

"Here, I think you will like this," Lucas said handing Amanda a glass of wine.

Later, desert was even better than the wine.

26

Chapter 3: Sao Paulo, Brazil

Anna loved December. She was second generation Brazilian. The family always got together at Christmas and celebrated around the tree in the German tradition. Her grandfather had emigrated from Germany after World War One.

On Christmas Eve the activities started with gathering around the tree and signing Christmas songs. Then after some treats and small talk each person got to select one present to open. Christmas Day everyone had breakfast and then gathered around the tree to sing some songs and open up the remaining presents. Christmas in Brazil had no snow. Until her medical school experience in the US, Anna had never seen snow.

The most interesting memory Anna had of Christmas in Brazil was the Christmas her father's sister brought German chocolate Christmas tree decorations.

Her mother kept everyone out of the living room. She personally decorated the Christmas tree and wanted to surprise everyone. It was to be a truly big a surprise.

Everyone was led in and stood singing Oh Tannenbaum in the dark. They were all were charmed by the candles burning in the tree. The flickering lights added a wonderful counterbalance to the black of the room. After the singing the lights came on and everyone let out gasped.

The chocolate decorations were melting, and an almost a foot wide stream of army ants were attacking and eating the chocolate decorations.

Suddenly the tree caught on fire.

Her father threw the water from the fire bucket at the tree and ran to get more water.

Anna clutched and tried to comfort her crying mother.

Her aunt went running about giving orders for more water. The fire was quickly put out.

That experience brought laughter in later years but as kids they had all cried because they missed out in eating the chocolate Christmas decorations.

Anna grew up as a tomboy. She fondly remembered her giant Eucalyptus tree. It was a meter in diameter and at least forty meters high and it had four major branches. The center branch rose almost straight up. Even a gentle breeze would sway this very top branch.

She was the only kid in the neighborhood who had braved the climb to its very top. To this day the memory of reaching the top inspired her. The wind swayed her back and forth as she let out her joyful cry.

The far horizon beckoned her.

It was like being in heaven.

From that day on the giant Eucalyptus tree became her tree.

About midway up the tree was one of the few branches that had grown out almost parallel to the ground. It was this branch where Anna would spend many an hour reading, doing homework or just daydreaming.

It was where she would go to get away from everyone and dream her dreams.

Anna's other pastime was riding through the woods and countryside on her horse, Kuti. This was her brother's nick name that she had purposely given to her horse to irritated him. She and a close friend were always riding out on some adventure that they would craft in their imagination.

The three families in the area lived at the foot of the mountains. This provided them with a huge area to ride and play.

They found the caves and some fortified areas left over from the revolution of various antigovernment fighters and the government soldiers.

They made up their own version of what had transpired in these spots. Of course, there were heroes and the heart break of lost love. They would ride in to change the course of a battle, or they would intercede to make sure two lovers would be united. They owned their fantasies, and they were some of the main actors and characters.

By the time she was twelve Anna was as tall as she was ever going to be. At the time she thought she was big.

She was definitely the toughest of her friends. She beat back every bully who challenged her.

As the years went on, she became the shortest of the group. Five foot two was it. The boys she had fought with were a good head taller, but her spirit and tenacity always let her win. Her early years had conditioned all the boys to fear her.

Many of the boys also wanted to be her friend so they usually gave way and helped her handle those who challenged her.

Anna grew up having a long shadow, high self-esteem, and ample self-confidence.

Her father was a mathematics professor at a small local university. He spent time each evening to review Anna's work and to encourage her. This was not hard since Anna was so competitive.

Her mother could never find Anna when housework was to be done. Anna felt guilty for a long time about not helping her mother. She was always surprised that her mother never found her as she sat reading up in the branches of her Eucalyptus tree.

Years later her mother had shared she had watched each time Anna climbed the tree. Her mother admitted to having been jealous that her daughter had found such a perfect place to dream. What was housework compared to dreams?

Anna excelled in her high school classes. She was active in the school social scene. Her easy nature and her acceptance by the faculty helped her get connected and accepted by Univerisdade de Sao Paulo.

The news of her acceptance was cause for celebration at home.

Anna was ecstatic. She would not be the first girl in her family to go to college, but she was determined to be the first one to graduate.

She chose to live on campus in the girl's dorm. It was a magic time for her. The world opened new doors. Her mind was challenged, and her social life came into being. Anna made friends easily and she was always organizing a get together for her close friends. Her parties always featured something special and became a draw for many other students.

All her life she had dreamt of love and romance, but the reality provided by the friends that got married convinced Anna that she had things to do before any romantic commitment.

She was enamored with the possibility of travel. The school had great connections with universities around the globe. Since these foreign universities were trying to attract students from other countries, they all waived their application fees. Anna applied to dozens of universities in the US, Britain, Portugal, Italy, France, and Germany.

She figured she had enough language skills to make it in any university in these countries.

Only a few schools offered her entrance and only one offered her a scholarship. Her family could not pay for her to go to school abroad. The scholarship was the key to a new world. She accepted a medical scholarship to Case Western Medical College in Cleveland, Ohio.

Anna shared the news with her family.

"Where in the world is Cleveland," her father exclaimed as he said, "No."

Her mother listened and said, "Go."

It was one of the few times Anna saw her mother exert her will and win.

Her father took it all with a grain of salt.

"Ah, if I could have had only sons," he moaned when he finally accepted the inevitable.

Anna immediately sent in her acceptance to Case Western Medical College.

Anna researched how to get to Cleveland. She could have simply taken a flight from Sao Paulo to Atlanta and then on to Cleveland. Instead, she found a freight ship that carried six paying customers from the seaport in Santos to cities in Brazil and then on to New York.

She chose the sea route. It was a much longer way to go but it would be a trip with many great stops to explore.

Once again it was her mother that came to her aid to convince her father.

The entire family accompanied her when she went to the cargo pier in Santos where the MSC Geneva was berthed. She was of German registry. That fact made her father feel better. The Geneva carried only six paying passengers.

The family came on board and were impressed with the room. Anna had chosen the smallest room that was listed as having 27 square meters of space consisting of a bedroom with private facilities, a shower, and a separate sitting room. There was also a small refrigerator, a television and video system. Anna immediately fell in love with the blue curtain and furniture covering theme contrasted against the rose wood finish on all the exposed wood.

Normally the ship only made two more port of calls in Brazil and then it would go on to the US. Anna had selected this particular time because the ship was scheduled to stop at several additional ports. For the same price as flying, she would visit four major cities in Brazil, visit the countries of Suriname, Guyana, and Venezuela. And also see Miami, Savannah, Charleston, Norfolk, and New York City and have a little spending money to boot.

Before disembarking from the ship, her Mother gave her an envelope. After the family had left Anna opened the envelope to find more than a thousand dollars in one hundred-dollar bills.

Anna looked about the room, felt the love her parents and brother had for her and sat down and cried.

Anna and the four other passengers spent the afternoon getting some safety training and shipboard rules explained. They were scheduled to have dinner with the captain. This was in the main ship's mess as a table set especially for them.

The Captain, dressed in official uniform, greeted each of the passengers and guided the talk so everyone had a chance to introduce themselves.

Anna listened politely. The young, noticeably in love newly married couple were Lara and Thiego Alves. The white-haired couple, James and Judy Mercer were two American's now on their return leg of their trip.

Anna introduced herself with a smile and an invitation to the rest to join her when she was visiting the various city ports that the ship would make.

The ship left the port during the early morning the next day. Anna watched the shore recede and finally disappear. The sun let her know they were traveling North. Vitoria the capital of the state of Espirito Santo, about a solid twenty-four-day sailing, was to be the first port. The ship was scheduled for three days of unloading and loading cargo.

The passengers were free to do as they pleased.

Anna spend much of the day sitting on a deck chair, in the shade reading. The expanse of the Atlantic and the solitude and quiet gave her a feeling of tranquility.

It was after breakfast the next morning that Anna caught the first glimpse of the coast on their approach to Vitoria.

The Geneva slowly approached a bridge that crossed the bay in front of them. Anna could see the morning rush hour traffic making its way across the span. To Anna's right she could see across into a harbor bordered by a continuous tan sand beach. Vitoria's business area also seemed to be situated to the right-hand side.

Anna marveled at the precision guidance the ship seemed to be given. It proceeded past one of the largest solid stone boulders Anna had ever seen. The boulder protruded out of the ground at least one hundred meters.

At this point the ship, with the help of a small tug made a one hundred eight-degree maneuver and moored just passed the foot of the boulder.

Anna took a taxi to the Art Museum where she spent a leisurely two hours. This was not enough time, but she wanted to go on to the Sao Gucalo Church.

She got out of her cab and looked up the three flights of marble stairs to the church with its two corner towers, a figure of Jesus with outstretched hand at the roof peak that rose to half the height of the two towers and the white cross silhouetted against a dark stained window that detailed the last supper rose before her. She made her way up the steps and entered to find one of the most gorgeous churches she had ever been in. She felt the height of the nave ceiling to seemingly shrink her in size.

Once she had walked halfway to the alter, she turned and gazed at the stained-glass window with the light of God highlighting a kneeling Christ. It was not the last super as she had thought it would be. She turned back toward the gilded alter and admired the organ pipes rising behind the alter.

She took several pictures and added that to her collection that she would be sending home.

Then she walked out and took a taxi to a Churrascaria for dinner. She paid for only the salad bar and had sushi, a sliced tomato and palm heart salad with blue cheese.

She returned to the ship with a bottle of Moscato and a couple of mangoes, a bunch of bananas and a box of chocolates. She planned to spend a quiet night with a glass of wine, a book, and the occasional chocolate.

The evening went by as she got into the story and enjoyed the wine and chocolate.

At breakfast, the next morning Lara and Thiego asked if they could join her to go shopping at the Capixaba craft market. There Anna purchased a variety of small native made craft items that she planned to give to the new friends she knew she would make in Cleveland.

The third day James and Judy joined the group, and they all took a half day bus tour around the various small cities making up the greater metropolitan area.

The ship left port early the next morning on its way to Fortaleza, capital city of the state of Ceara. There the unloading and loading routine was the same.

Anna led everyone to the beach. Later in the evening they all went out to enjoy the dancing and night life. The next day was spent sleeping on the beach and once again it was the night life.

Anna would have liked to have spent more time on the beach and night life, but the ship was once again on its way after the third day.

Standing on the bridge and watching the ship head out to sea gave Anna the feeling of adventure. She imagined what it must have been like to be standing on a wooden deck looking up at sails filled with wind and moving out into the unknown and to possibly ferocious storms.

The next port, Belem, was at the mouth of the Amazon River. Anna was amazed at the size of the mouth of the Amazon. At Belem she could not see the other bank of the river. The muddy brown water made a brown strip several hundred kilometers out to sea. The captain informed her that the discoloration of the sea could be seen from space.

The stay in Belem was to be of the same duration as the other ports.

Lara suggested a trip to the Vero O Peso market. Everyone agreed on that destination and Anna suggested they also visit the Emilio Goeldi Museum that had a world-famous collection of the artifacts from the Amazonian Region. The tour book also highlighted several good restaurants near the museum.

Anna suggest the Market, lunch, the Museum followed by dinner. They could decide on the after-dinner activities during the day.

Everyone had a good time at the market. Anna again selected a few items as gifts. She loved the museum and the history and information about the people of the Amazon.

Anna learned more about the Amazon in the one visit then she had learned anywhere else. She decided she would come back on the following day.

Anna's invitation to return the following day was rejected by Lara and Thiego who were planning a bus tour of the city. John and Judy agreed on another visit to the museum but suggested a half day bus tour for the afternoon.

Anna countered with doing a half day boat tour.

In the end everyone chose to get back together to take the boat tour together.

When the ship left port, Anna was once again pulled into her fantasy pirate, sea world. The ship was now bound for Miami and would be at sea for the next several days.

The meals on the ship were great and the sailors all catered to Anna's every need. Every evening the five passengers would all gather to talk, drink some wine, sing, and play cards.

They were often joined by some of the young sailors. There were only sixteen members of crew, and they enjoyed interacting with Anna and the other guests.

Anna made a point of being friendly and of politely rejecting the marriage proposals that were thrown her way on a daily basis.

It was a trip of a lifetime. Anna was really happy about her choice.

In Miami it was the beach and a little night life. Miami was more expensive then she could afford, and she was glad to move on.

Savannah and Charleston were more to her liking, and she took several bus tours and visited a few museums.

The Navy base tours were interesting in Norfolk, but the beach was a disappointment. Anna had been spoiled by the beaches of Brazil. Her visit in Norfolk was OK.

The panoramic view of New York at night, as the ship made its way to the dock, imprinted itself on her mind. The Statue of Liberty with the lighted torch light that flickered off the black surface of the water was magnificent.

Anna recalled all the stories her grandfather had told about his disappointment when his visa to the US was not approved and why she was a Brazilian instead of a US citizen.

The night skyline, the Empire building in all its splendor and the high-powered beams blazing into the night sky commemorating 9/11 where the twin towers once stood, the Verrazano bridge outlined by white lights connecting Manhattan to the New Jersey side.

What a glorious place.

Anna stood on the deck above the ships bridge with her shipmates. She listened and all of them took turns pointing out the wonders in appreciative whispering voices. She looked over to see tears in John's eyes.

Lara and Thiago suggested that they take in a Broadway show together as their last outing together.

Anna quickly suggested they go see Wicket. The ship's steward had let her know that he could get her discount tickets. She was happy when everyone agreed. She had come to realize that it was hard to fully appreciate such events when at the end you had no one to share your impressions with.

Her time in New York was short. She said goodbye to Lara and Thiago. They agreed to get together when Anna returned to Brazil.

James and Judy said their goodbye's and gave their home address and telephone number and invited the three to keep in touch and if they were ever in Iowa they should stop by.

The next morning Anna boarded a Delta flight to Cleveland.

She took a shuttle bus from the Airport to the Case Western campus.

The clashing building styles, and colors and the campus layout made Anna wonder what mad scientist or color-blind designer was responsible for the mismatch. Every building seemed to be out of place. Some seemed to have been dropped into a commons area in a moment of confusion.

Later it all grew on her, and she became accustomed to the lay out and to the friendly atmosphere she enjoyed there.

Coerced and pushed by her new friends, Anna became a fan of American football. They insisted she learn how the game was played. One of her new friend's father gave his daughter, Rosemary, and Anna a pair of season tickets to the Cleveland Browns games. These were tickets to enclosed box seats. Anna wondered how much such tickets cost but was afraid to ask.

Anna at first didn't understand the game and was constantly asking questions of clarification. By the end of the first season, she was hooked.

Later back in Brazil she would hold parties where she streamed in the football games on her computer.

Rosemary invited Anna to spend the summer at her family cottage. It was located in the upper peninsula of Michigan. Anna could not afford to travel to Brazil for the summer and was thrilled by the invitation.

She drove up to the cottage with her friend Rosemary.

The cottage was right on the beach of Lake Michigan.

This was the first time Anna experienced a freshwater beach. The beach was not great by Brazilian standards and the water was very cold by the same standards. But the morning swims were invigorating and the walks to warm their blood back up always prepared them for a hearty breakfast.

Time seemed to accelerate to the speed of light. She went to sleep one night only to find out it was time to return to school.

Anna loved her time in Medical School. She studied hard. She made great friends and she fell in love with the atmosphere and flow of life in the United States.

She entertained thoughts about immigrating to the US. She was one of the top ten graduates in her class and figured that she would be able to land a job in the US.

She was placed on the list of available doctors and given several areas in the US where she would be able to get a US visa so that she could practice medicine in the US.

She could have accepted a position in almost any hospital in the world, but she decided to return to Brazil and take a position in a hospital close to home.

Once again it was Anna's mother who helped her makeup her mind. Her mother put her in contact with a family friend who was now a hospital administrator. He convinced Anna that she was needed in Brazil. She would just be another doctor in the US. In Brazil she would make a significant contribution to the people of her country.

Anna accepted a position at Hospital Municipal de Diadema in Sao Bernado Do Campo.

Anna thought about going back by sea, but she realized the magic of her trip coming to the US was the magic of the first time. Trying to repeat great moments and experiences was often disappointing. Time was now more pressing, her trip to the US had taken forty-five days. Her trip back to Sao Paulo took seven hours.

Anna spent the first few weeks reconnecting with her old college friends. She was quickly reminded of her father's saying, "time changes everyone and new water constantly passes under the bridge. Nothing stands still."

Marta, Anna's best childhood friend. Her horseback riding partner and participant in their make-believe romances and other adventures, had attended a few years of college. Marta dropped out to get married. She was now a mother of a cute little three-year-old boy, Rolando. Marta and she remained friends but the two of them did not have much in common at this stage of their lives.

After Marta's several match making attempts failed, Anna was aware of getting invited over usually only for Rolando's birthday parties or major family events. She was told that she was Rolando's favorite "Aunt."

Anna understood and was somewhat relieved Marta had stopped trying to play match maker. Marta's choices of suitable partners just did not meet Anna's specifications.

Thiago and Lara, her friends from the trip to the US by ship, were friendly but they now had two children and were consumed being good parents. They lived in Sao Paulo and were generous with invitations to dinners at their home.

Anna once again found that she enjoyed being with them, but it would only be at those times that she could participate in what the family was doing.

Suzanne her best Brazilian college friend had taken a job in Rio and was the buyer for women's lingerie for Victoria's Secrets. Their reconnect had been joyful.

They were both single, successful young women. Suzanne and Anna shared a similar energy. They were always cooking up the next thing to try or to do.

Currently, of the two, Suzanne made more money, but Anna could afford the outings and parties they shared.

Anna on the other hand had the more prestigious job title. They both enjoyed playing this out when they went out on double dates.

Suzanne set up and provided sizzling dates. Her picks were always aimed at a good time out and a good time in.

Anna did her best at lining up good dates, but her selection came from a different more serious stock of doctors focused on their careers.

As it turned out this was a perfect arrangement. Suzanne slowly became serious with one of the young doctors Anna set her up with. And Anna enjoyed playing the field and did not have to be concerned about being committed.

Twice a month they got together. They agreed to split their outings between Rio and Sao Paulo. This allowed them to share the cost of the travel between the two locations.

This morning Anna was in the hospital cafeteria taking a break. She groaned as she looked up from her reading.

Orlando Cardoso, another young physician at the hospital was coming toward her table. He had been hitting on her and just would not take no, as an answer to his advances.

Anna had arranged one date between Orlando and Suzanne. He was a good doctor but self-centered and a bore. After that date, Suzanne had put in her stop order. Orlando was dropped from the list. Somewhere along the line he must have decided to try for her.

She tried to telepathically transmit a loud NO don't come to my table. It was clear to her that she had no telepathic power.

"Hi, Anna, can I sit down for lunch with you," Orlando asked?

She looked at her watch and was relieved to see she had only about ten minutes left before she needed to get back to the emergency room. She turned down Orlando's invitation for dinner and fled toward the emergency room. It was one of the few times she looked forward to her time in the emergency ward.

A few hours later she was on the train to Rio. She went to the dining car and ordered a beer. The waiter behind the counter recognized her. She had taken the train back and forth often enough that she knew many of the workers and conductors by name.

Later Anna shared her most recent encounter with Orlando as she relaxed in the easy chair in Suzanne's living room.

"So, you got away from him again," Suzanne said, "you really deserve a break."

Anna replied that she indeed needed a break. She was going to start taking walks instead of reading in the cafeteria.

"Well forget about him. I have two hunks lined up that you will love. They are built, they are well to do, and they are eager to go to the beach with us tomorrow afternoon and to party all night long as well. Get ready to rock," Suzanne said as she raised her mug of tea like a drink.

"Yes, I am ready, and I have my string bikini along. I just hope that I am in good enough shape to raise my date's libido," Anna replied.

48

Chapter 4: Muri

*H*e was Muriuki Lamand. His Friends called him Muri.
Muri's family had moved from Kinshasa in the western part of
the Republic of Congo to the city of Pweto at the very eastern
border of the country in order to escape the strife from the
turmoil generated by what his father termed "the African World
War." Pweto, located on the edge of Mweru Lake, seemed to be
the place to escape the violence occurring in the East. Later the
family found out that it did little good since Pweto ended up
being another center of conflict.

Muri quickly adopted Pweto as his "Home." He remembered
only a little about his life in Kinshasa.

He had many friends. His best friend, John Mustafa born in
Pweto, and he were inseparable. They were always on some new
adventure that they together had cooked up.

Pweto with a population of twenty-four thousand was small
enough that Muri and John quickly explored every conceivable
building they could possibly play in.

When the army chose to position armed troops in Pweto, the Lamand and Mustafa families joined with ten other families to move out of Pweto to a location down the Luvua River.

Muri remembered taking the ferry across the mouth of the Luvua River as they started their journey to their new home. He and John were riding on the back of one of the motor bikes as they traveled south on the N5 for about five kilometers. Their journey then took them north, Northwest along a small dirt path. It started out as a road but quickly became nothing more than a path. Twelve families, moving single file, traveled parallel to the Luvua River for more than twenty kilometers.

Muri hoped that their guide actually knew the way. By the third day he was sure they were lost. The only constant was the river.

On the third day they reached the location selected by the leaders of the group. Muri's father was a member of this group. They had previously scouted out this location and received official permission to settle on the land.

All the families were Catholic. They had made the move in part because they were concerned, they would be singled out by the troops that were of different religions.

The location proved to be isolated enough that marauders or renegade fighters did not bother to come their way.

Muri and John helped build a strong stockade in the center of the village. The group had enough fire power to effectively fight and hold off any attackers.

Muri and John quickly familiarized themselves with the country around them. The lush green strip along the river gave way to a drier almost barren land as they got farther away from it.

They traveled the river downstream through rugged stone covered terrain, interspersed with brush and trees growing out from every crevasse.

It was a challenging environment but one they embraced immediately. They ventured to hunt small game and when faced with a bigger danger they were quick to climb or run to safety.

Muri remembered the first time they had discovered the great falls, their favorite swim hole, and the cave with drawings all at the same location.

Muri found the cave only because of the fascination he had with the large crack in the face of the cliff. His curiosity was fueled by the fact that there was a huge rope anchored at the top of the steps leading down to the bottom of the waterfall.

Who had put the rope there?

Then when he got to the huge crack, he crawled up the slope of stones wondering what he would find.

The cave was dark, and it was impossible to tell how big it was. He and John had made a torch out of some grasses and pieces of wood and had discovered that the cave was just high enough for them to stand up. The discovered drawings on the back wall done in white and black of someone fishing and another one of someone fighting with a lion.

Muri and John decided they would take their Christmas vacation at the falls and use the cave as their place to sleep.

They brought their camping gear and enough food to last them for at least a week.

Muri and John arranged their belongings into four bundles that they could carry down the steep steps to the base of the cliff.

The cave and the falls were their destination.

John climbed up the slope made by loose stones and put the cooler with food into the cave. Muri contributed the sleeping gear. They returned to the top and brought back the remainder, including their kerosene lamp and lantern.

After arranging their belongings, Muri declared their Christmas vacation was officially started.

Muri declared that it was time to swim and the two headed for the river.

Muri and John got to a branch in the path. One branch led down to the river, the other to their diving and jumping spots. Muri stopped John as John turned toward the jump off spot and pointed toward the river.

John acquiesced and agreed that he was too excited and followed Muri down toward the river.

They went down to the river and swam to the swim hole.

Muri had learned to check out their jumping spot for debris or fallen rocks. There was always something coming down the river. They had once needed to take out a small log they found going around and around the pool but never quite making its way out.

Then there was one older person in their small village who had told them how he had jumped in and hit a submerged log in a similar situation. He broke his arm and collar bone. His collar bone had never heeled properly and to this day his left side was almost useless.

Muri did not want to end up like that.

They found the swimming hole clear. After almost an hour of a continuous cycle of jumping in and swimming, John suggested they go fishing so they would have something fresh to eat for dinner.

Muri was eager for a good supper but was already hungry and suggested they tide over their hunger and eat one of the treats his mother had sent.

Muri and John carried their fishing lines, a supply of hooks and walked down the river path to where they had hidden their poles the last time, they had gone fishing.

After sitting on the riverbank and eating their snack they tied their lines to their poles and baited their hooks and began to fish.

Muri complemented John on the two nice sized fish he had caught. He was about ready to give up when he realized he had a fish that felt like a rock. He realized his line would not be strong enough to pull the fish directly in. Instead, he walked along the bank up stream to a shallow rocky area.

John called out in surprise when he saw the size of the catfish. Muri knew they would not need to fish again. This one fish would be enough to last them for the week.

Slowly and patiently, he pulled the catfish up through the shallow water into the rocks. John whacked the fish several time in the head with the back of the ax. He then left to cut a long skewer pole on which to place the fish for cooking.

The fish took up almost the entire length of the skewer. It was the biggest fish either of them had ever caught. It was at least fifteen kilos in size.

Together they carried the fish up to the cooking fire ring. They cleaned all the fish, collected wood for a fire   and began to cook.

John made one more trip to the cave to get the cooler. It was the only container they had large enough to put the fish into. He also carried back the lantern. It would soon be getting dark, and the large fish still needed more time to get fully cooked.

Muri lay back taking in the millions of stars in the dark night sky. He and John were lounging by the fire as they continued to cook the fish. It was the Solstice.

They had three more days of fun along the river before they needed to be home. They knew they had plenty of food and their days would be spent swimming, jumping, and hiking along the river.

The two lay on their backs pointing out and discussing the various constellations and stars in the night sky.

Finally, the fish seemed to be done. Muri raked the hot coals to one side and John put the cooler on the other side. They cut the fish into sections that fit into the cooler. Three of the four sections fit in the cooler. The tail section was more than the cooler could hold.

They each ate one of the small fish and then ate a small piece of the Catfish.

"Let's have an evening snack," John said, as he filleted the meat off the tail section and gave half to Muri.

"It sure tastes delicious," Muri commented as he took his first bite. The only spice they had used was salt rubbed on the skin of the catfish. After they ate their fill, they both fell asleep by the fire.

It was still dark when Muri woke up. He nudged John awake.

Together they carefully negotiated their way along the crack up to their cave. After getting everything inside, they pulled the rocks up to the cave mouth and sealed the entrance.

They were almost immediately asleep on their sleeping blankets.

Chapter 5: Cualli

Cualli ran ahead of Tosi as they raced to get to the bus carrying the group to Chichen Itza. He and Tosi were the lead players in the re-enactment of the sacrifice of a virgin to appease the Mayan gods.

This was somewhat a perversion of history since it was the Aztec that had done most of the heavy duty sacrificing of maidens and captured enemy warriors. But the re-enactment was about the business of attracting the tourist and making money.

The name of the area meant "At the mouth of the well." It was one of the Seven Wonders of the World. The current modern name was probably not what the area or city was originally called. In its day it was a city with economic power and a trade route that extended both into North and South America. The Mayan kingdom was at its height around 600 AD.

It had a known "city center" of around five kilometers and most likely had "suburbs" out well beyond that. It had stone paved roads.

Their show utilized the four-sided Temple of Kukulcan, also known as El Castillo at the center of the city. It was believed to have been built sometime around the tenth century.

Cualli had learned that there were ninety-one steps on each side. Counting the last step to the top platform as one and adding it to the sum of the four sides, yielded three hundred and sixty-five. This was the three hundred sixty-five-day calendar year!

There were fifty-two panels on the pyramid. This corresponds to fifty-two weeks!

These facts had captured both Tosi's and Cualli's imaginations. They had always imagined the calendar as being defined in Europe!

Sculptures of plumed serpents decorate the northern balustrade of the temple. During the spring and autumn equinoxes the sun struck the northwest corner of the monument and the shadows it created the illusion of a feathered serpent. This alone was enough to draw in more than a million tourists.

The Tourism and the dollars it represented was the reason for the current virgin sacrifice reenactment. Virgins were sacrificed by the Mayan but at a location other than the top of the pyramid. It made for a much better theater to place the re-enactment at its top.

Tosi played the virgin and Cualli played the high priest who cut her throat and ripped out her heart.

Tosi and Cualli met two years before on their first day of Class at the Universidad Nacional Atonomo de Mexico. Cualli asked her out as they walked out of their first class. Tosi knew immediately she was in love with Cualli.

They had dated ever since that first day. They got along great both as friends, as collaborating students and as lovers. They were meant for each other. Their friends all saw how well they got along and agreed.

Cualli was from Apizaco, Tlaxcala. Tlaxcala was the smallest of all the Mexican states. He had a large family and was the first to attend college. He was the oldest. His family had put all they had into him. He worked hard to get top grades and had received a partial scholarship.

To make ends meet and not put any additional financial load on his family, he worked on a variety of jobs. He worked as a waiter on the weekends at the Marriott to make enough money to stay in school. In his current role as the high priest, he could not work at the Marriott, but the manager had told him to let him know when his role as priest came to an end. He could have his job back.

This had been a great relief. The role as priest paid twice as much as his role as waiter but it was seasonal and would come to an end soon.

Tosi was from a well to do family. Her father was a manager at a manufacturing plant at the Naucalpin plant. Her older sister had graduated and was now working as a new manager at the at another manufacturing plant in Mariscala.

Tosi hoped she would be able to get a job with a company as good as her sister had.

She had done OK in high school but knew she did not have the same drive and intensity her sister had. She was still searching for the field of study that would capture her imagination.

She knew it was not a matter of intelligence because she had outscored her sister academically, but she did not have the deep desire and work ethic she saw in her sister.

She and Cualli had competed and won the contest to be the virgin and the high priest for a series of shows for the tourists. She did not need the money but knew it was important to Cualli.

They joked that they had found the serious work that they planned to pursue for their livelihood.

The "virgin" was led up the ninety-one steps of the pyramid and sacrificed to the gods to prevent any catastrophe from happening. The show was performed through the fall and would end on the Solstice. Each show ended in a fireworks display. The final display on the Solstice was to have a grand finale and a party afterwards. They anticipated the biggest crowd for that last show.

"I'm glad you're having fun playing the virgin. I won't tell if you don't," Cualli said with a grin.

Tosi commented on how much fun it was to be playing the virgin.

They were running because they were late for the bus. They had been in bed messing around until the last possible moment.

They had lost count of the number of shows. The show consisted of about two dozen players dressed in traditional Mayan costumes. The music was a mix of drums and guitars with a steady processional beat.

The procession marched in and slowly climbed the steep narrow steps up the side of the pyramid.

An announcer would tell the story over the loudspeaker. Cualli and Tosi never said a word. Once the procession got to the top, Tosi was placed on the stone alter and Cualli "sacrificed" the virgin to appease the gods and held up her pulsing heart for the audience to see.

The tourists willing to pay the extra fifty dollars were spectators at the top. The rest were gathered down below around the base of the pyramid. There were always around a thousand people.

The realism always caused the audience to let out a gasp and then explode in applause.

"I'm sort of sad tonight is the last show," Tosi said with a sigh.

"So am I," Cualli replied.

Cualli was thinking about the after the show love making. Tosi got worked up being the virgin and he got worked up trying to please her afterwards. Cualli thought it was a great arrangement.

He hoped there would be other occasions where they would have a similar experience

The money he had made would pay for his tuition and books for the following two semesters. Most of the money came from tips the tourists gave he and Tosi.

Tosi always tried to give him her share, but he refused. He wanted to keep their relationship on a level basis.

He might not have as much money in his family as Tosi had in her family, but Cualli was proud of having a connection back to the time of the Aztecs. His first name meant good in the Aztec language. He had the common Mexican family name of Gonzalez.

The Spanish had converted ninety five percent of the native population to Catholicism. He knew his family was of the mestizos' class in Mexico, but he had researched his family as far back as he could, and he was certain he really was linked with the Aztecs.

Cualli had been following the research and studies of the Zapotec prophecy found in the Eagle bowl. It had an inscription that read, "After thirteen heavens of decreasing choice, and nine hells of increasing doom, the tree of life shall blossom with a fruit never before known in creation, and that fruit shall be a new spirit of men."

This year was especially important since the Aztec calendar predicted some major, potentially catastrophic events.

This had many interpretations by experts pointing out the recent events that were supposedly predicted by the prophecy and other Aztec calendars and documents.

December twenty first was the end date of the five thousand one hundred twenty-six-year Mayan long count calendar that coincided with the Aztec calendar and for some technical reasons more exact on the calendar time.

Experts predicted a variety of events ranging from a great cataclysmic event to a spiritual alignment of the human consciousness.

The astrologers all pointed to the alignment of the planets, the moon, and the sun.

Some scientists pointed out the abnormal swing of the poles. None of the experts seemed to be able to be certain about anything.

"What do you think tomorrow will bring," Cualli said as he waited for Tosi to get on the bus ahead of him.

"Hey, the virgin finally came," someone on the bus joked.

"That's why were late," Cualli joked back.

"You're terrible," Tosi said as she sat down and poked him in the stomach.

Cualli commented that he thought the coming catastrophic Event prediction was being pushed by hucksters trying to cash in on the public's naivety.

"It's been fun playing the sacrificial virgin at Chichen Itza," Tosi replied.

It had been fun, and it was an easy way to make some extra money before Christmas. She and Cualli both needed the money to buy their family some small gifts. She knew Cualli was also counting on the money to continue in school.

Tonight, was the last series of shows. They would do three sets. Each would end in fireworks.

The last show was set for midnight.

Chapter 6: Lucas, Buchanan, Virginia

Thanksgiving had been great. He, Amanda, Rachel, and Jeff had gone out several times on some double dates.

It was great to see that Rachel and Jeff seemed to connect with each other. Lucas was not surprised. Jeff was really quiet an intellect and the two were the same age. Rachel had chosen to stay until the very end of her vacation.

He had come with Jim, Evelyn, and Clair to the Roanoke Regional Airport to see Amanda off. Lucas watched as Amanda walked to the security line. She was eager to get to her new job in New York.

Amanda was just starting out. He knew she was currently focused on her new role as a financial advisor at EA Whittely LLC. She excitedly described her new role as a financial advisor. Lucas did not discourage her, but he had a friend who had taken that route and got burned out in about two years.

Lucas kept quiet. Anything he said could be misconstrued.

He worried about their age difference but there was nothing he could do about how he felt when she was around.

"You two seem to be a pair," Evelyn commented as she waved to Amanda who was leaving the security area.

Lucas replied that Amanda would certainly be on his mind in the coming weeks and hoped that he was the one she wanted. He knew that Evelyn had been working on the match making. He appreciated her support, but he was aware of the ten-year age difference between him and Amanda. It made no difference to him, but he was sensitive about Amanda's old man comments.

Lucas felt as if he were saying goodbye for the last time. He figured it would be a long summer.

Rachel, Amanda's friend was still in town and was staying with Jeff. The two had hit it off and seemed to be getting started on a real romance. Rachel was going to New York as well and would be sharing an apartment with Amanda. She had another week before she needed to be there and had chosen to spend it in Buchanan with Jeff.

"I am so excited about having Rachel stay. She is even interested in how we run the paper," Jeff had shared with Lucas.

Lucas joked with Jeff about Rachel's personality and gave him a pat on the back when Jeff just smiled and said thanks for choosing me.

It seemed clear to Lucas that he did not have the same connection with Amanda.

Lucas concentrated on his architectural work, the garden, and his animals. The month went by amazingly fast. Tending the garden, raising the chickens and rabbits took up most of his time.

He was making almost as much money from selling "Organic" vegetables, "Naturally" raised rabbits and chickens and large brown eggs as he made from the architectural work.

He was recognized in the paper for his donations of food to the local charities.

Evelyn and Jim were fully supported by his garden, meat, and eggs. This was Lucas's continuing college fund gift for Clair.

Before he knew it, June evaporated.

The Fourth of July was spent with Jim and Evelyn. They once again went to the Roanoke Airport to take in the fireworks display. It was the first time for Clair. They arrived in the early afternoon. There was a fair like atmosphere to the celebration. Lucas had a great time buying Clair, a hot dog and later some cotton candy.

"You know you spoil her. Every time you come over you bring her a gift. Every time we go out you buy her what she wants. When we say no to her, she always says she is going to ask Uncle Lucas," Evelyn teased.

Lucas was very careful to check everything with Jim and Evelyn to make sure they approved of just how much he spoiled Clair. He really did enjoy spoiling her. And he liked being called Uncle Lucas by her.

At the end of the fireworks, Jim was carrying a sleeping Clair back to the van they had all come in. They had about a forty-minute ride back home. When they came to his lane, Lucas jumped out at the foot of his drive.

"You sure you don't want me to drive you up," Jim asked.

"It's a nice night and I'll enjoy the walk. Thanks for inviting me to come along," Lucas replied as he got out and closed the van door.

He walked up the lane toward the house. He was thinking about Amanda. He really liked her, but he felt there was something between them that had not clicked into place. It bothered him that he seemed to be the one who had doubts about their relationship.

He had talked to Amanda about once a week since she left. She was not planning to return until Thanksgiving.

He wondered if they would still be a pair by that time

He took in the stars in the night sky. He turned to look down the mountain to the valley below. He was content with himself. He was a little lonely but not desperate.

Time will tell he muttered to himself and went into the house.

It was a saying his mother always used when there seemed to be an unanswered question or problem.

For the rest of the summer Lucas kept busy at his job and in taking care of the homestead. July, August, and September went by swiftly.

His garden gave a bountiful yield, and he had the cool room filled to the brim.

His rabbits also had a bountiful year, and his chest freezer was also full.

His friends also enjoyed his success, and the churches all sent a thank-you card to him.

His sales of rabbit meat had soared, and he was in great financial shape.

Lucas successfully kept himself busy as he navigated his tenuous love life.

Once a month he would go have dinner with Jim and Evelyn. Lucas volunteered to take Clair trick-or treating in Buchanan.

"You are welcome to come with us. This is Clair's first time to go, and we are not going to miss it," Evelyn replied when Lucas made the offer.

Lucas immediately accepted the offer to go trick or treating with them but invited the family out to dinner at the Rhine River Inn before going trick or treating.

He had anticipated Evelyn's answer and already had dinner reservations. He planned to bring his camera and capture the event in both still shots and as a movie.

Evelyn accepted his dinner invitation. The dinner was great but everyone including Clair was eager to get on to the main event.

Watching Clair trick or treat for the first time was a treat for the three of them. Lucas, Jim, and Evelyn had a great time walking along and talking as Clair rushed up to the door and rang the doorbell. A few times Clair jumped back as the homeowner popped up in the doorway wearing a scary outfit.

"How many shots can you possibly get of the same thing," Jim commented as Lucas kept his Nikon clicking.

"I'll edit them this weekend and send you the treasure of a lifetime," Lucas replied.

He would reduce the thousands of shots to the top fifty or so and then he would arrange them in a story or timeline fashion.

Lucas looked forward to crafting the story. He planned to make it the center of entertainment for all to enjoy after the Thanksgiving dinner.

After trick or treat was over, he was dropped off at the foot of the lane leading up to his house.

His thoughts turned to Amanda. Lucas sensed a change in their relationship. Amanda had become polite and proper in their conversations and the frequency of their talks had dropped off significantly.

He wondered whether they would last until Thanksgiving.

The following three weeks seemed to crawl. There was now silence coming from New York. Amanda did not answer Lucas's last two calls.

He decided to let things be. Mentally he began accepting the change in relationship and that what he had dreaded had finally occurred.

The week before Thanksgiving, Evelyn took Lucas aside after their Friday night dinner.

"Lucas, Amanda is bringing a friend with her. She is a little afraid of how you will react. This is a guy she started to date about a month ago," Evelyn said and then stopped.

An empty feeling went through him. He knew it was over just as he knew it had never really been. Lucas was not surprised. It fit with the change in the discussions on the phone and then the silence.

Amanda evidently did not know how to handle it herself and did not have the courage to speak her mind openly to him, so she had leaned on Evelyn to be the bearer of the news.

Lucas felt that Amanda was a dear, but the two of them had not made the deep connection that Rachel and Jeff had found.

It hurt but Lucas had no hostile feelings. She would always be a bright point of light in his mind.

"I'll be OK. I won't hit the guy with a baseball bat if that is what she is worried about," Lucas said jokingly to Evelyn.

"We still want you to come for Thanksgiving dinner. I just wanted you to know ahead of time, so you didn't find out when you came in the door," Evelyn whispered as she gave him a hug.

"Yea, thanks for the heads up. Tell Amanda she should have done this herself," Lucas replied as he finished his beer.

Jim came by and just patted him on the shoulder. Evidently, the two had talked about it and Jim had decided he was not going to be the messenger.

Lucas was glad that he had hiked over for dinner. He figured if he cried all the way home, he would feel better in the morning.

Lucas had volunteered to cook the turkey.

He followed his mother's recipe and carefully basted the turkey until it was a golden brown. The stuffing was made out of sweet potato, celery chunks and chopped almonds mixed with several tablespoons of brown sugar. This stuffing was one of his favorites.

Lucas drove his truck loaded with a variety of vegetables in the bed and the aluminum foil covered turkey on the passenger's seat.

He almost dropped it as he took it in and came face to face with Amanda as he went into the kitchen.

Amanda stepped aside to let him pass as she said hello.

Lucas put the turkey on the counter and told Amanda how glad he was to see her.

He wanted to take her in his arms and hug her, instead he extended his hand.

Amanda took him by the arm and pulled him into the family room where her new interest was talking to Jim.

"Let me introduce you to Ned," Amanda said.

Ned and Jim had been talking. As Amanda led Lucas into the room, Ned stood up to shake hands.

"Pleased to meet you, Amanda has told me a lot about you," Ned said as they shook hands.

Lucas wondered what Amanda might have said about him. Hopefully, just that he was a good neighbor and friend.

He smiled and made the usual introductory reply.

He was not pleased to meet Ned but was not about to say it.

Lucas found the situation a little awkward and uncomfortable.

"I was just asking Ned which teams he thought would go to the Super bowl. Why don't you get a beer and join us," Jim spoke up?

Lucas thanked Jim and turned to go to the kitchen to get a beer. He was not planning on joining them anytime soon.

He had brought over a basket of both sweet and regular potatoes and some acorn squash. He also had a small pumpkin. The chicken and rabbit had been delivered the weekend before. Most of the Thanksgiving dinner was from his garden and homestead.

He quietly walked out the front door.

Amanda followed him out to the truck.

"I'm sorry I wasn't brave enough to tell you myself. Evelyn told me what you said. I was afraid it might spoil your friendship with them. I really want us to be friends," Amanda said as they got to the truck.

It was hard for Lucas to reply. He knew in the long run they would never be friends. They would interact in a friendly manner when they occasionally met.

"I have thought about this a lot. You're a bright point of light in my mind. I can only wish you well and hope you find what you are looking for. Even if I were to hate you, my friendship with Evelyn, Jim and Clair are based on my interactions with them, not with you," Lucas replied quietly and calmly.

He was anything but calm. He was fighting to control his primordial instincts.

He took the DVD from the seat of the car and gave it to Amanda to carry.

He was having trouble with his emotions. He wanted so much to hug and feel Amanda's soft curves. He had not expected such intense feelings to surface.

He took the basket of potatoes and led the way back in carrying the pumpkin on top of the potatoes.

"You're a dear," Evelyn said as Lucas entered the kitchen with the pumpkin.

She looked at both Lucas and Amanda. She could tell Lucas was trying to escape the moment.

"Amanda, Clair just asked where you were. She wants to show you her new dress.

"Lucas, do you mind helping me for a moment," Evelyn said as she strategically sent Amanda out of the kitchen.

She knew this would naturally separate the two.

"Are you OK," Evelyn asked Lucas once Amanda had left the kitchen.

Lucas replied that he was OK and confessed that is was just a little harder than he expected.

The rest of the afternoon and evening was a blur. Lucas and Jim chatted. Clair occupied Amanda while Ned sat quietly near them.

After the Thanksgiving meal, Lucas connected Jim's computer to the television and played the trick or treat DVD.

Evelyn was the narrator at the beginning of the pictures, but Clair quickly took over once they got to the trick or treat scenes. Her squeal of delight and periodic laughter carried the day.

Lucas sat back and enjoyed the whole event. He noticed Ned seemed bored. This secretly pleased Lucas who did not like what seemed to be Ned's superior attitude.

Afterwards they watched the Green Bay Packers beat the Pittsburg Steelers. It was time to call it a day.

Clair was already in bed sleeping.

Lucas said goodnight to Jim and Evelyn. He wished a good trip back to New York to Amanda and Ned.

Silently he said goodbye.

Lucas did not see Amanda after that. She left the day after Thanksgiving.

He did not know it at the time, but they would never see each other again.

She had plans to go to Ned's family's place for Christmas.

Lucas went back to his work and homestead routine. He continued to have an empty feeling.

It hurt enough that he almost wished he had not met Amanda. It had been a Thanksgiving-to-Thanksgiving romance, and he was the turkey, was his last thought on the subject.

<u>Chapter 7: The Party</u>

Lucas was out on one of his church vegetable delivery runs when he was presented with a gift by the one of the church deacons. The gift was a female puppy that was the last of a liter of pure-bred cocker spaniels. The church member had been very specific that it was to be given to Lucas for being so generous.

Lucas accepted the puppy and knew immediately who it was really going to belong to.

It would be an early Christmas present for Clair.

He took it directly to Clair. He figured if he took it home he might get personally hooked on the pup.

Evelyn and John thought it was a great gift.

Clair was ecstatic and spent every moment, "training" Lady.

It turned out Jeff and Rachel had connected, and a spring wedding was in the works. Rachel and Jeff sent him an invitation to a Solstice party at Pete's Pub and Grill. Lucas held the invitation in his hands and smiled. At least one of them had found their soul mate. He remembered how worried Jeff had been about going out on that first date with Rachel.

Lucas would have to remind him about the discussion of whether the date had a personality. There was enough personality that Jeff was planning to spend a lifetime with her.

He left early on his drive down to Buchanan. The lack of snow made Lucas realize it would not be a white Christmas. The weather had continued to be erratic. It was the solstice, and the temperature was in the high sixties. Places like Atlanta and Houston were getting snow. There was no indication of snow in the Blue Ridge Mountains. They had gotten a lot of rain instead.

He arrived at Pete's Bar and Grill way too early, but this meant he got a parking place on the curb in front of the door. Pete greeted him and led him to the back corner booth facing the door.

"What would you like to drink? The first one is on me. As a matter of fact, I owe you so much for all the food you have given me that you can drink all you want this evening and it's on me. Merry Christmas," Pete said.

Lucas asked for any dark or black beer.

"Sure, I'll be right back with it," Pete said as he turned back to the bar.

Lucas thanked Pete for his generosity and wished him and his family a Merry Christmas.

He appreciated Pete's generous thank you gesture.

Lucas concentrated on reading his book. He was on his second beer when an old high school friend came in.

"Well, if it isn't the mountain hermit himself," Sam said as he sat down.

Sam was now working in the coal mines. It occurred to Lucas that Sam was beginning to look older, and more worn than his years.

It also brought Lucas's Dad to mind. The conditions in the coal mines had improved since his day but it was still dangerous and continued to take its toll on the body. The thought about working in the dark and being fed bullshit brought a smile to Lucas's face.

"Hey, Pete, bring us two more of whatever Lucas is drinking," Sam called out.

Lucas thanked Sam but politely pointed out that he already had consumed two beers and needed something to eat before drinking anymore. He was trying to politely say no thank you.

"And bring us some nuts, potato chips or how about some of those onion straws," Sam called out.

Lucas would have preferred to continue reading but he put the book down.

Lucas knew Sam loved to talk about his basement survival chamber. He asked if Sam was ready for the talked about the EVENT.

"You bet, send it my way. You're welcome to join me if you get lonely on the mountain," Sam said and then launched into sharing his inventory of gear, food, and weapons he had accumulated.

Sam had added significantly to the things he had accumulated in his basement since the last time they had talked.

Lucas wondered what kind of world would exist if it was full of armed and dangerous survivors. It would not have surprised him if Sam claimed to have a missile launcher.

The cool room built into the bedrock protruding out of the mountain side at the homestead was what Lucas considered his survival chamber. It held the garden tools and recycled plastic forever tomato stakes on one end and the garden and canned goods on the other end. The freezer with all his frozen meat and some vegetables was also in the root cellar. Currently it was also the storage spot for all of Lucas's camping and hiking gear.

Together they finished the beer Sam had ordered.

Then in rapid succession friends, acquaintances and other partiers began pouring in.

Lucas went out and put his book into the truck. He almost left to go home but just then Evelyn, Jim and Clair arrived, and they all went in and sat down together.

Jeff and Rachel came in a short time later. Their faces said all that needed to be said when they looked at each other. They thanked everyone for coming and then they announced their engagement.

Pete had hired several of the local high school kids to help him cater the meal. The guests had the choice of grilled chicken or steak and a choice of red or white wine. Simple but good.

After dinner, the dancing started. About nine, Evelyn congratulated the bride and groom and thanked them as she and Jim left with Clair. It was time to get Clair home and into bed.

It was early and Lucas decided to stay for a little while longer.

Lucas was happy for Jeff and Rachel.

He was also feeling a little sorry for himself as he thought about him and Amanda. The beer glasses sitting in front of him began to pile up. Another keg was tapped, and the beer came even faster.

Somewhere along the line, Pete began bringing chasers to go with the beer. Lucas had not partied or drank so much since his freshman year in college. The last he remembered of the party was the wet T shirt contest Sam initiated with some of his other friends. When Lucas stood up to pour the first pitcher of water, he felt sick from drinking too much. He turned and went outside instead.

His truck was parked in front of him. He remembered getting in, but he had no clue how he got up the mountain to the homestead.

Lucas woke up. It was almost pitch black. An old flashlight with a faint yellow glow of batteries about to expire lay at his side. He was not surprised to find himself in the cave. This had always been the place he came when he had been drinking as a teenager.

He used the remaining anemic light to find his old kerosene lamp. He found the lamp and finally found his spark generate stick that he used to light the lantern.

Lucas looked around at the mess in the cave. He must have been in an uncontrolled rage if he had somehow overturned and throw every object in the cave around in the helter-skelter way, he now found it.

As he turned the electrical generator to its upright position, the sharp pain in his right side made him stop and look into an old mirror. Not only was he feeling miserable, but his face was also covered with blood. The source was a gash on the top of his head.

He realized his head was pounding. His right-side pain seemed to come from his ribs. And he had abrasions on his hands.

He righted his old rocking chair and decided to sit down and take stock of his situation. Whatever fight he had been in; he must have received the worst end of the beating.

He would need to go to the house and get himself patched up before cleaning up the mess here in the cave.

Lucas turned toward the cave entrance and stopped when he realized the blackness outside the cave was not the night but a sheet of solid water. It was not just raining but solid things were falling from the sky. He could not make out any of the homestead buildings. There was only a solid sheet of water.

He was glad that the cave floor sloped from a high in the back downhill to the cave entrance.

He stopped short. He had never seen rain like this. No, it was more like a solid sheet of water. It was not just raining but solid things were falling from the sky.

He found an old towel and held it out in the rain to wet it. He began to clean himself up. The rainwater seemed brackish, more like saltwater then rain.

He was disoriented. He was trying to make sense of the situation.

Lucas did what he always did when he was stressed. He began to straighten out the cave. He found his reserve food and sat down on his rocker as he ate one of the power bars. He looked out at the solid wall of water and with terrifying clarity he realized that the Event he and Sam had been joking about had happened.

He wondered how long the water could continue to fall at such a rate.

Lucas knew he could make it to the house with his eyes closed because he had done it many times when as a kid, he had decided he wanted to know how it felt to be blind.

He knew by heart that it was one hundred sixty-three paces in what he thought of as a minus ten degrees from the straight line out of the cave mouth.

He closed his eyes and walked out into the rain. The rain was so dense he found it hard to breath. He stumbled downhill toward the house. He fought the almost knee-high torrent of water that was pushing him toward the house.

He thought he had counted his steps wrong because he did not find the edge of the porch as he had anticipated. He tried looking but he couldn't see a thing. The rain was too dense.

For the first time, Lucas felt fear. He needed to get out of the deluge before he drowned in the standing position.

Lucas continued his forward progress. It was lucky that he was walking with his hands out before him because he felt the cold wet granite that he knew was directly behind the homestead.

Lucas thought he was lost. He could feel the rock but could not see it or his hands!

Logic told him that he was against the granite that formed the outer wall of the cool room.

Panic screamed that this was impossible.

He was lost.

Lucas felt first to the left and then to the right. As his right arm extended to its limit, he felt the edge of cut stone. He moved over to his right until he could feel the door handle. A shiver went through his body. He knew he had his hand on the door to the cool room located in back of the house. He slowly lifted the handle and opened the door.

Lucas stepped in and got out of the rain. He closed the door and stood in the dark.

He took several deep breaths. He was shivering, not so much from being wet but with the realization the home he had grown up in was missing. The words, "The house is gone." was frozen in his mind.

The house was gone…gone!

Lucas knew that his survival hinged on gaining control of his emotions, taking stock of his situation. He had enough food in the cool room to last him for a very long time and Lord all the water he could possibly ever dream of needing.

It was pitch black in the cool room. This room had always fascinated Lucas. Unlike most rooms where one's eyes picks up just enough light to see, the darkness of the cool room was an absolute black.

Lucas slid along the wall toward his left toward where he knew his camping gear was located. He periodically squatted and let his fingers do the seeing. He carefully organized the objects he found.

Finally, his hand touched the old lantern. The glass shield was broken. He hoped the nylon bags were still functional. He knew he could light the lantern even if they were broken.

He spent the next few moments that seemed to be an eternity trying to find the lipstick sized match container.

Lucas spent three precious matches getting the lantern lit. It gave a feeble light from its two broken illumination bags.

He found the other three lanterns and the kerosene can. He was thankful that he had followed his father's advice on always closing the cans.

One lantern had a cracked glass and the other two had no damage. All needed new illumination bags.

He repaired the three lanterns and pumped up each lantern and then he used a piece of broom straw to light the bags as he turned the knob to let the pressurized spray come into the sock. Each of the lanterns provided additional light.

He looked around.

The cool room was a jumbled mess similar to the cave. Luckily, the shelves holding the canned food had not come apart. Earlier he had left the retaining bar off one shelf. The glass on the floor was from the one of few jars that had fallen from the shelf. The other eleven shelves were properly barred, and everything was intact.

Lucas surveyed the rest of the room. It looked as if everything had been randomly tossed about. The freezer was miraculously up right though it had a dent in the top where it had hit the light fixture on the ceiling.

Lucas took the broom and swept up all the glass. Next, he made sure the emergency electrical generator was functional. He would not start it until he was sure he could open the door to let exhaust fumes out of the room.

The freezer would be good for several days.

He made quick work of straightening out the rest of the cool room. His Dad had designed and built each one of the shelves with a holding bar to keep things from falling. If he would have been following Dad's rule of always putting the bar back after taking an item off a shelf, nothing would have been broken.

Lucas opened the door to see if the rain was letting up. It was still a solid sheet of water. He wondered how Jim, Evelyn and Clair were doing. He hoped they were OK.

He found his cell phone in his pants pocket but there was no reception.

He found it unbelievable that his house was gone.

He now wondered about his injuries. Was he tossed around in the cave like the stuff in this room? Had there been an earthquake, a tornado? What had happened?

By this time Lucas was a little paranoid. He knew where he was, and he felt totally helpless and unprepared to handle the situation.

He wondered what had happened down in Buchanan. What had gone through Sam's mind as he faced the end? Had it flashed through his mind that it was not supposed to happen in that manner?

He hoped that Jeff and Rachel had been embracing when the end came to them.

For a moment he wanted to call out to his mother. He let out at little hysterical chuckle. It was true, you always cried out for your mother at the moment of need.

88

<u>Chapter 8: Anna</u>

Anna's, Rio friend Suzanne lived on the twelfth-floor apartment on R. Decio Vilares Avnuet. Suzanne came from a very well to do family and lived the lifestyle to which she had become accustom. The location, the apartment with at least twelve hundred square meters and its decor was what you would see in the magazines when looking at how the rich and famous lived.

This evening the two were sitting on the roof deck savoring a glass of Merlo and enjoying the view of the Sugar Loaf out to their right. They were taking turns looking through binoculars at the Giant Statue of Christ, Christo Redentor on the mountain top out to the right.

The two had toured both of these Rio attractions on previous outings. Those were what Suzanne referred to as proper events. This weekend was to be the naughty event.

Anna was ready for something on the wild side and Suzanne assured her that it would be one of the better weekends they had so far shared together.

Anna and Suzanne dressed in short, shorts and white mid-drift sleeveless blouses drew a few wolf whistles as they walked the seven blocks to the Coca Cabana beach.

They met their dates, Victor, and Mateus at the beach. Suzanne knew them both from the gym where she worked out each day.

Suzanne had invited them to the beach, and they had suggested an evening of dancing after a dinner.

They got in some beach volleyball, walked down the beach and along the famous black and white swirled promenade. The four sat in the shade and slowly sipped on their beer as they discussed what to do that evening.

Anna who loved to dance suggested a light dinner and some dancing.

Suzanne seconded this. She then suggested they do their dancing on the roof of her apartment building where a small live band was performing.

Anna with Victor and Suzanne with Mateus walked the seven blocks back to the apartment. On the way a small corner restaurant attracted Suzanne and they all ate a light meal.

The four returned to Suzanne's apartment. Both Suzanne and Anna chose to take a quick shower before going dancing on the roof.

They danced until Suzanne led her date back down to the apartment. Anna followed with her date.

After filling their wine glasses, they each led their dates into their individual bedrooms.

It was four in the morning when Anna was awakened by her watch. The room was dark but the light in the bathroom blazed a bright vertical slash in the darkness.

Anna groaned inwardly.

She would have loved one more round with Victor, but she needed to get dressed and catch a cab to the train station.

She was the trauma surgeon on duty and needed to get back to Sao Paulo by eight.

She quietly got up and got dressed. She kissed Victor lightly on the cheek and whispered "Obrigado." Then took the elevator down to the lobby. Her cab was waiting for her. She would make sure to have Suzanne arrange more dates with Victor and Mateus.

She was happy to get to the train ticket counter. There was no line, and she was able to immediately buy her ticket.

She knew the train was almost ready to depart. She boarded the closest car and began to walk forward toward the car where her seat was located.

Anna was ravenous and when she got to the dining car, she decided to get a strong cup of coffee and a sandwich to eat. She ordered three sandwiches. One for immediate consumption and the other two for when she was on duty.

The train had just started to move when a surge of people seeking coffee came into the dining car.

Anna sat down on the bench seat with her back to the windows and put her coffee on the round table with a single center leg. The surge of coffee seekers subsided and finally she and another couple were the only ones to occupying the dining car. She nursed her coffee and ate the warm sandwich she had purchase.

The windows on the opposite side were still black. The sun was not yet ready to warm the day.

Anna let her mind wander over the events of the weekend. The click clacks of the train on the track seemed to slow her thinking and lull her to sleep.

The coffee was gone. The sandwich a pleasant remembrance. She was about to get up and get a refill for her coffee when suddenly she started to float out of her seat.

Her immediate reaction saved her. She pulled herself under the table and held tightly to center post.

The world seemed to be going crazy.

The couple sitting across from her were not as fast. They floated to the ceiling and were helplessly pinned there.

Anna felt guilty about not responding to the lady's call for help but there was nothing that she could figure out to do.

When Anna saw her breath, she realized how cold it was getting.

She crossed her legs with the table leg at its center. She used her sweater like a rope and tied her torso to the leg as well.

All she could think about was that the train had been in an accident. But there had been no braking and no impact. Nothing seemed to make sense. She felt weightless.

All Anna could do was to hold on to the post. She found it hard to breath. It got very cold. Then she lost consciousness.

Anna regained consciousness and was totally disoriented. It took her a moment to remember that she was on the train. It was pitch black and she could not see a thing. She was still gripping the table post. It was raining outside, and water was running past her along the floor. She felt around and realized the car was at an angle. The bench seat was behind her.

As she moved to get on the seat, she screamed from the pain shooting up from her leg. Her hands found the bone sticking out and she let out an involuntary moan. She knew she had a very badly broken leg.

She felt to see if there was any arterial bleeding and was relieved to find none. Through the pain she pulled herself into the V formed by the angle of the bench seat.

She passed out.

She came to sometime later. It was still dark, and the rain had not stopped. She was still disoriented and in great pain. Her leg was now throbbing and even though it was cold she was sweating.

Anna knew she was in grave danger. She struggled to make sense of the situation.

Her hunger trumped the pain.

She felt around trying to find the sandwiches that she had purchased. She found one wedged under her head. She remembered her mother giving her a hard time about picking up dropped food and eating it. She could not see the condition of the sandwich and it did not matter. She was so hungry she didn't care where the sandwich had been or for how long.

She gobbled down the sandwich and then passed out again.

When she came to for the third time the pain was excruciating but she was determined to help herself. It was still pitch black or it seemed to be. Slowly her eyes made out the objects in the room. The rain was loud as it poured down on the dining car.

She knew she was in grave trouble. She hoped the rescuers would get her out of the train in time. She would not survive many more hours on her own.

She could make out what seemed to be two crumpled bodies about six feet away. They were not moving. They appeared to be dead. Anna recalled seeing them being slammed around the car before she had passed out. She called out to them but there was no response. There was no way for her to check on their condition.

She saw several wrapped sandwiches on the floor.

She found a random round bar of stainless steel and used it to work the sandwiches toward her. There were four well wrapped sandwiches. They appeared to be undamaged. She ate one immediately and placed the other three above her head.

The pain in her leg was bearable as long as she did not move. Once again, she hoped the rescuers would come soon. The ceiling of the dining car seemed to have been compressed down to the bottom edges of the windows. The window now looked to be only a few centimeters high.

This time fatigue and pain pulled Anna into a deep sleep.

She was delirious when she came to again. It was still raining, and water was now running along the bottom of the bench seat. Anna was dry up in the bench seat. The angle of the car made it appear it was a V for channeling the water.

She decided she needed to take some first aid action. She sat up and bent over at the waist. She slowly reached down with both hands and wedged her foot under a fallen bar located at the end of the seat.

She thought about her yoga teacher's coaching about doing things slowly and carefully.

She wished there was someone to help her take the next action.

She braced herself and slowly and continuously pushed herself upward along the bench seat. Her long continuous scream filled the cars enclosure, and it was the last thing she heard as she passed out.

Anna did not know how long she had been out. She felt better. Her hunger let her know she had been out for a long time. Now she was very cold. She ate her third sandwich. She had only one more left.

It was still raining. She could not hear anything but the rain falling on the dining car and the water rushing passed her on the floor.

At least now she could make out her surroundings.

She located her purse and recovered it with the help of a steel rod. She retrieved her scarf. She took the lip Vaseline she had for her lips and applied it to the jagged gash that was just below the knee. She then wrapped the wound tightly with her scarf.

She moaned at the pain but kept herself from passing out as she applied the bandage.

Anna was trying to figure out how long she had been on the wrecked train.

She had eaten three sandwiches. It was more than minutes. It was probably many hours. She had passed out three times. So, the time could be in days. If it was days, then either the rescuers could not get to the train, or they had given up hope of finding anyone alive.

Anna decided her survival was up to her.

She decided that she needed to make some noise. She took up the steel bar she had used to retrieve her purse and began to tap out help in Morse code. .... . .-.. .--.

After the second time she cursed "para o inferno com ele" and just banged continuously back and forth in the slot made by the compressed window frame.

Chapter 9: Muri

*M*uri woke up in the dark cave. He could barely see the morning light that struggled to penetrate the crack in the cliff face and get to the opening of the cave. He wondered what time it was and knew he had only slept for a very short time.

Both he and John remained on their sheepskin sleeping mats as they quietly talked about what they would do for the coming day.

They had planned to do a lot more fishing but the huge catfish they had caught was all the food they needed.

There was no reason to get up early so they chose to chat and snack on some of the fish they had grilled.

They discussed just doing more swimming and diving. They discussed that floating down river would also be a good idea.

Muri closed the cooler and was putting a piece of the fish into his mouth when he suddenly was slammed against the ceiling. The cooler also hit the ceiling just missing his head. John had cried out when he hit the ceiling. Muri had blood running into his eye from a cut in his scalp. John was moaning in pain from his experience.

John was repeatedly asking what was happening. Muri had no idea what was happening, and he had no answer. All he knew that there was some force holding both he and John to the ceiling.

He looked over at the cave opening and was amazed to see that the massive rock that formed the wall on the other side of the crack was gone. He wondered how that was possible.

The light was not normal but appeared to be grey.

Muri told John to look out the cave entrance.

John wanted to know what he was supposed to see.

Muri was so engrossed at the missing rock that he overlooked their predicament of being pinned against the ceiling.

John complained about not being able to breath.

A few moments later Muri passed out.

Muri came to. He felt groggy and tired like when he had run a long distance at top speed and run out of breath. He felt his head and realized the blood on the cut in his scalp had coalesced.

He realized that some significant time had passed.

He realized that he was laying back on the floor of the cave.

He recalled being slammed onto the ceiling, now he was back on the floor of the cave. He looked around in confusion.

The cave was dark, and it was hard to see anything. When he looked at the cave opening, he could only see what appeared to be water.

He called out to John.

There was no answer, but he could make out John laying on the cave floor.

He crawled over and rolled John on his back and called his name. He checked John's pulse. He was alive. Just out.

A few moments later John slowly recovered.

"Where am I? What happened?" John asked as he looked at Muri.

Muri responded that they were in the cave but added that he had no clue what had happened.

They crawled over to the cave opening. All they could see was a curtain of rain.

John did the same and then commented that the water tasted more like salt water than fresh river water.

Muri tasted the water and agreed with John.

Muri commented about the missing section of rock and about the fact that the water tasted like salt.

"Remember the talk about the end of the world. Maybe this is it," Muri speculated.

Muri remembered his parents talking about the end of the world. He speculated that perhaps this was how it ended. He hoped that his parents were OK.

John commented that they were lucky to be alive.

We need to find out how the people in the village are doing Muri commented.

He realized that they would need to wait until the rain stopped. Muri hoped it was rain and that the river had not re-routed itself to fall down over the cave. If it was a river reroute he figured they were toast.

Muri suggested they eat and then decide what to do next and when to do it.

Muri took a long stick he had found and went to the mouth of the cave and tried to find how far down the ground outside happened to be. He knew that the slope up from the entrance to the crack to the cave mouth was close to ten meters.

The stick was about two meters in length. Even when he stretched as far as he could the stick did not hit anything.

We have a problem Muri declared. Its going to be a long way down to where we will be able to stand.

The cooler was banged up, but the latch had held. The three section of fish were in good shape.

Muri and John organized and packed all there camping equipment as they waited for the rain to subside.

They discussed the problem of getting out of the cave.

Muir lit the wick of the old lantern. The lantern glass shield had shattered. He and John collected all of the broken glass and put it down a crack in the rock. They both agreed that getting more cuts would make things much worse than it already was.

The fumes from the lamp made the air in the cave a little thick.

They moved all of their belongings close to the cave opening and then turned the lantern off.

Muri suggested they make a rope from their sleeping hides. They took turns cutting the hides into strips of leather.

John was the better weaver so as quickly as Muri cut leather strips, John would weave them into the rope. The going was slow and tedious. However, neither of them cared. There was on other choice but to get the rope done.

Muri examined the final product and complimented John on the quality of the woven leather rope. He added that he hoped it would reach to the ground.

John thanked Muri for the compliment and then added that now they did not have a sleeping blanket. He hoped that the rope would get them out of the cave and on the way to the village.

He voiced his concern about their families and the rest of the villagers. He asked the question how high he thought things outside might have been pulled. He pointed out that they had been slammed against the ceiling and that stopped them and finally they had run out of air.

He asked, "What did the people in the village experience? And if the event had lifted the huge boulder, had it lifted the buildings of the village?

The same concern had been in Muri's mind, but he had refrained from asking. A frightening realization had flashed in his mind. John had been right about their time on the ceiling.

What if they had been out on the riverbank? What would have stopped their upward flight?

The rock in front of the cave was gone. Was their village still there?

"I am glad the ceiling in the cave is as low as it is. We might not have survived in one with a higher ceiling," Muri commented.

John nodded in agreement. He had come to the realization that there would be no village.

John and Muri looked at each other. There were tears in both their eyes. They had both come to the same realization.

Muri reached over and gave John a hug.

"We have each other, and we will survive," he whispered.

Little could either of them imagine what the future held in store for them.

<u>Chapter 10: Cualli and Tosi</u>

Cualli lead the procession toward the pyramid. This was the very last enactment of the season. There would be a grand finale this evening and the cast would have a party later.

Tosi was dressed in a shear white outfit. Even though she wore a bikini under her outfit, she loved the fact that her outfit was somewhat revealing and sexy. For the third time that day they climbed up the narrow steps of the pyramid and made their way to the sacrificial altar. The thirty or so tourists paying extra for the privilege were gathered around the altar. Four of the escorting guards picked Tosi up, held her high and then placed her on the sacrificial altar.

Cualli smiled at Tosi and whispered, "This is the last time I get to stab my favorite virgin."

He raised his knife to simulate cutting her throat. He was suddenly totally disoriented. He reached down and pulled Tosi to him, together they flew up into the sky. They were not alone. Everyone and everything were flying up and away from the ground. Everything was flying up, the whole pyramid and the audience around the pyramid.

Cualli took the long white robe Tosi was wearing and tied it twice around the two of them. Tosi was absolutely silent and clinging to him with her legs wrapped around his waist. He passed the robe below her legs, so she was tied securely to him.

"It's the Event. I love you," Tosi whispered and kissed him on the neck. She was sure they were not going to survive. She was happy that Cualli had tied them together.

Cualli could feel himself getting lightheaded and it was getting colder. When he looked down, he could see they were now over open water and moving very fast both upward and out over the ocean.

But something was very wrong.

The ocean was also coming up toward him as well. All around him people were screaming and moaning. The large stone altar of the pyramid was still near them.

Cualli put his feet on the altar and pushed away as hard as he could. The altar he was sure weighed several tons. He was glad to see he and Tosi rise up faster than the altar and all the people around them.

"Tosi, I love you. I don't know whether we are going to live through this. I am glad I have you in my arms," he whispered.

Tosi just pressed her lips to his and gave him a kiss and then put her cheek to his and hugged him tighter.

Cualli was struggling to keep breathing. He told Tosi to try and hyper ventilate like they did for long distance swimming.

The air was thin, and it was slowly getting colder. He wondered how high they had gone.

His push off the altar continued to separate the two of them from all the other objects coming up with them. He could barely make out the other people. He felt like superman.

"We are very high," Cualli commented.

Cualli spoke in a very low voice as they continued to rise up into the sky, "What goes up must come down he continued. If we don't come down, we will freeze in space. If we come down, we are like eggs falling off the table."

Suddenly they were gasping for air. Tosi passed out first. Cualli felt her arms let go. He was glad they were tied together. He pulled her arms in between the two of them.

He just finished tying his hands together behind her back with the tail of the robe when he passed out.

Cualli was dreaming of having to get up for school. He tried to get his mother to stop calling his name.

"Let me sleep, I don't have school today," he blurted out.

"Cualli, Cualli, please wake up," Tosi kept saying as she lightly slapped Cualli on the cheek.

"We are on the way down and I am scared," Tosi whispered in his ear.

Somehow this penetrated Cualli's mind.

Suddenly Cualli came to and pulled Tosi to him.

"Where am I," he said in confusion and then it all came flooding back to him.

He looked down. There was nothing but water below them, but the water was not too far away, and it was moving down with them.

He immediately knew that there might be one chance for them to survive. They needed to hit the water below them like a spear. Once they hit, they needed to surface as fast as possible.

He untied Tosi and told her to stand on his feet and tie their ankles together. He then tied their waists together.

"How long do you think we went up," Tosi asked.

"I think just a few minutes," Cualli replied.

"Then we probably have only a few minutes to live," Tosi murmured.

"Let's do some deep breathing and hyperventilate," Cualli instructed.

"God grant us a miracle," Cualli said as he put his arms around Tosi.

Yes, they were most likely going to die but if they landed in water, he wanted the chance to live. He knew he could dive and resurface from at least sixty feet of water. He had no idea where he was landing but there certainly was a lot of water around him. He saw no land.

Suddenly they hit the water hard, but it was not the extreme impact he had anticipated. It was more of a smooth continuous plunge. The plunge seemed to be endless.

He was struggling to figure out which way was up when his feet hit something solid. The last thing he remembered before losing consciousness was kicking off the bottom with all the strength he could muster and taking several strong strokes to propel them upward.

Tosi could feel Cualli stroking and then stop. She continued on for at least four more strokes before she too passed out.

"It's not so bad," was her last thought as she swallowed a mouthful of water.

Water falling on his face, water pushing on his body and water choking him brought a choking, hacking Cualli back into the world.

He suddenly realized Tosi was limp in his arms.

He felt for her pulse. There was none. His adrenaline kicked in.

He untied her from him in superhuman speed. He pulled, carried, and dragged Tosi up toward the beach.

He started mouth to mouth resuscitation as he carried her and stumbled as far up the beach as he could then he hung her from his shoulder with her head down and squeeze her chest so the water in her lungs would run out.

Finally, he laid her flat, gave her air and pumped her heart.

He lost track of time. He took up a rhythm of two deep breaths, five heartbeats: over and over and over.

He was crying, pleading with God, promising everything.

The rain continued to fall; the water was rising.

In desperation he pounded on Tosi.

"Please, Please, Please," he repeated over and over.

Suddenly Tosi opened her eyes, grabbed his hand, and tried to talk through a coughing fit.

"Ouch," Tosi finally got out as she sat up.

The rain was still pouring down. They sat holding each other. Cualli was crying. He couldn't help himself.

Tosi just held his hand.

"I thought I had lost you," he whispered in her ear.

Cualli led Tosi up away from the water. The rain made it impossible to see where they were going. They had gone up about twenty feet along a trail when they came across a stranded dolphin.

"How in the world did the poor thing get up here," Tosi reflected.

"The same way we are here," Cualli responded, "Let's see if we can move it down the path to the water."

They seemed to be on the top of a rise. It was downhill in both directions. Cualli was disoriented. He did not know which way they had just come. He walked down the slope and came to water. But it was not as violent as he and Tosi had just escaped.

Together they slowly pulled and pushed the dolphin down to the calm water. The dolphin seemed to know they were helping it and wriggled as they pushed and pulled. After about an hour they accomplished their good deed.

Once in the water the dolphin took over and swam away.

"Ok let's see if we can find shelter to get out of this," Cualli shouted through the pouring rain.

The hard work with the Dolphin had invigorated their muscles but Cualli could feel the cold robbing him of the warmth the hard work had generated.

It seemed like the rain was getting colder. He was now becoming concerned about suffering hypothermia.

Just past and to the left of where they had found the stranded dolphin, they found not so much a cave but more of a large overhang. The floor slopped up toward the back. There was a fair amount of debris. Some old coconuts, palm leaves and pieces of wood were all piled up at the back.

It was good to get out of the rain and the huddled together at the back of the cave.

"Let's see if any of my Boy Scout survival skills become useful," Cualli said as he gathered the materials to make a fire.

He shredded an old palm stalk into some fine fibers and made a loose ball of them. He found a hard-straight stick and a piece of wood to act as the friction point. He put the fine fiber around the friction point. He hoped to have a small fire in a few moments.

"I'll clean out an area back here so we can sit down. I wonder if any of the coconuts are still edible," Tosi said as she began to clean up. She put all the coconuts into three piles: old and useless for food, probably edible and too young and green.

Outside the rain continued to pour.

Tosi watched as the fire lit. She was wearing only her string bikini and hoped that the fire would warm the two of them before either of them got any colder. She carried over a variety of material to feed the fire. She hoped old coconuts made good fuel.

Chapter 11: Clair

Clair was awakened by Lady. Uncle Lucas had given her Lady. He had brought Lady over in his backpack and asked her if she wanted what was inside.

She always said yes. Uncle Lucas always had great surprises.

Uncle Lucas always brought her a surprise in his backpack. She loved getting the surprises and she loved Uncle Lucas. Lady was the best surprise she had ever gotten. She gave him a big hug and kiss and then sat playing with her new puppy.

"You're now her official hero," Evelyn said as she leaned in the doorway frame leading into the kitchen.

Evelyn and Jim had agreed a dog would be a great gift.

"What are you going to call her," Jim asked from the couch?

"She's Lady," Clair declared.

She had watched the Walt Disney movie Lady and the Tramp and loved both dogs. It was her favorite movie and she watched it at least once a week on tape.

"Well, you continue to be the best neighbor we ever had," Evelyn said giving Lucas a big hug and kiss.

"Thanks, she is a good-looking dog," Jim chimed in.

Watching Clair with her new friend was all any of the three needed to know it had been a good decision.

For the next couple of weeks Lucas came over and helped train Lady. It was really an excuse to come over more often and spend time with Clair and the family.

The holidays were hard on Lucas. He had always spent Thanksgiving and Christmas with his Mom and Dad.

Amanda had moved on and once again he was alone.

After returning from the Solstice engagement party for Jeff and

Rachael, Evelyn, and Jim put a sleeping Clair to bed and put Lady at her feet.

"That was a good engagement party. Those two seem to make a perfect pair. I guess Lucas is better at matching up pairs than I am," Evelyn said as the two walked back into the family room.

"You know, I think Amanda goofed by letting go of Lucas," Evelyn went on. "He is such a good guy,"

"Oh, quit being a match maker. I agree with you, but Amanda's got to follow her own course. I know that is what Lucas thinks as well," Jim commented.

He personally thought Amanda and Lucas would have made the perfect couple, but he knew it didn't matter what anyone thought. He had only had a few beers because he knew he had to drive up the mountain to get home, but he was tired.

"Let's go to bed and get some sleep," Jim said leading Evelyn back to their bedroom.

Later that night Lady began whining. She licked Clair on the cheek until Clair came awake. Then Lady ran to the door and began scratching it to get out. Clair groggily followed lady to the door and opened it. Lady immediately ran out into the night.

"Come back, come back, Clair called quietly. She didn't want to wake up her Mom or Dad. She knew she wasn't supposed to go out by herself at night, but Lady was out there, so she went looking for her.

"Lady, Lady," Clair called and wandered farther from the house.

She heard a scratching noise near the storm shelter. The shelter was really nothing more than a small cave that had been converted into a storage area. It was where her mother kept the extra food supplies. She had also put in some stormy weather supplies and old clothes.

Except for the stars in the sky, it was pitch black.

"There you are," Clair said to Lady as she knelt to give her a hug.

Lady continued to scratch at the shelter door. It was a long reach for the latch cord to the shelter, but Clair stood on her toes and pulled the cord. The door swung open, and Lady rushed in.

Clair followed.

"What's the matter Lady? Where are you," Clair called out?

The whining came from the far corner of the cave shelter. Lady was under the bottom shelf of the built-in shelving.

"Why are you acting so weird," Clair asked as she tried to pick Lady up.

Lady moved farther away from Clair. Clair had just crawled under the shelf so she could reach Lady when the door slammed shut and she was slammed into the bottom of the shelf above her. The shelf moved up and hit the one above it. There were a series of these small slams. Clair was shaken but not really hurt.

"Mommy, Daddy," Clair wailed as she clutched Lady to her chest.

She heard strange cracking and breaking sounds outside. She was pinned against the bottom of the top shelf. Clair could not see it but everything in the shelter was up against the ceiling.

Clair began to cry.

"I think the wicked witch is coming," Clair whispered to Lady as she remembered the scene out of the Wizard of Oz.

Lady licked Clair's cheek and she felt better. She fell asleep with Lady in her arms.

The next thing she knew she slammed against the floor. She had a cut on her forehead and was bleeding. Lady licked her scratch.

"Yew, Thanks but let me get a hanky," Clair said as she sat up.

She was now too scared to cry.

It was still dark and now it was raining. She went to the door and looked out. She couldn't see anything. The rain was a solid sheet of water.

"Mommy, Daddy," Clair called out as loud as she could.

She was no longer afraid of getting into trouble. She was now just afraid. She wanted her parents. Something weird had happened and she was afraid. She was glad to have Lady in her arms. Lady licked her face again.

Clair turned back into the shelter. She was cold and it was very dark. She went to where she knew the bed was. It was a mess and not exactly flat. She crawled up on the mattress. After pulling the covers over herself and Lady, she said a prayer and slowly went to sleep.

Mommy would find her in the morning. She hoped that she would not be mad.

Chapter 12: Up the Trail

ℒucas kept the door partially open to the outside. Periodically he would sweep out any water that had splashed in. He was now getting a tiny bit of light from outside.

He realized he had been walking back and forth.

He ate a tomato and pulled a pickle out of a jar and took a crunchy bite. Pickles were his thinking snack food.

He wondered about Clair, Evelyn, and Jim. Lucas decided he needed to get up the trail and make sure they were alright. He became more worried about them as he paced back and forth waiting for the rain to subside.

His house was gone. It had been well built but it was gone. He wondered about Evelyn and Jim's place.

He looked out into the rain. It still looked like a solid sheet of water but at least the falling objects seemed to have stopped.

Lucas decided to hike up the trail. It was only a mile but a mile in this weather was more like ten.

It took him three times as long to make the trek.

He packed a small backpack with some food and water and put on his rain gear. He didn't expect to stay dry in the torrent, but he wanted to prevent hypothermia.

Standing in the corner was his father's walking stick. It had the symbols of every trail his father had hiked. Lucas cherished it. He had started using it after his father passed away. He picked it up and carefully opened the door.

He was still amazed that his house was gone.

He walked out and made a large circle in the homestead flat. Everything was gone; the house, the two barns, his truck.

Once he relocated the door to the cool room, he was able to reorient himself. He would need to stay focused. He would be blind on the trail up to Jim and Evelyn's place.

It would be a blind man's hike. He could barely make out his feet. He chuckled to himself about the fact that he was a "homeless" blind man taking a hike across a challenging ridge.

He decided that if he survived this hike, he would carve an eye into his father's walking stick. It was the only thing that was keeping him on the trail.

Lucas found it difficult to find the trail head and then he found it even harder to stay on it. His landmarks all seemed to be missing. He knew it was early afternoon, but it remained dark making it hard to see and to keep track of time. He had to shelter his wrist up by his eyes to see his digital watch.

He knew his pace and he kept a close eye on the time.

It was about the time that he should be at Jim's and Evelyn's place. He stopped to get oriented.

Using his walking stick like a blind man feeling his way, Lucas explored the flat area he knew had been the location of the Evelyn and Jim's house. It was a repeat of his own place.

A sick feeling went through Lucas. If they had been in their house in bed, they were gone.

Tears were washed from his eyes by the unrelenting rain. He let out a loud scream and cursed the heavens.

Then he remembered the storm shelter. It should be ahead and toward the left. He nearly ran into the door when his walking stick hit it at its base. Lucas felt around and found the cord leading to the latch. He pulled it and stepped inside.

Silence greeted him. He immediately had a foreboding feeling.

"Jim, Evelyn, Clair are any of you in here," Lucas said slowly.

He was just getting ready to find a lantern when a small voice spoke up.

"Uncle Lucas is that you," Clair whispered from her bed.

She was sitting up looking carefully over the edge of her covers.

"Clair, where is your mom and dad," Lucas asked.

He was overjoyed to hear Clair. Tears welled up in his eyes.

"I don't know. Lady ran out here and I followed. Then we floated up to the ceiling. A little while later we fell to the floor. I think the wicked witch was here," Clair said as Lucas sat at the edge of the bed and Clair crawled into his lap.

I'm here and I'll take care of you. We will go see where your mom and dad are when it stops raining," Lucas lied.

He was certain they would be wherever the house had gone. That to Lucas meant they were dead.

Lucas used his flashlight to locate a lantern.

The storm cellar was well stocked with food. Evelyn had turned it into her pantry. She figured where better to store extra food then in the storm cellar.

Jim had copied the shelf design from Lucas's storage room. All the jars seemed to have survived. Most of the food was from Lucas's garden.

There was a fifty-pound bag of rice, a fifty-pound bag of black beans and about six cases of bottled water.

Everything lay around on the floor. It was lucky that none of them had hit Clair. There was also a variety of dry goods. There was lots of pancake mix and dried noodles that could be cooked in water. These were all goods that would store well for a long time. The room was well supplied but at the moment it was a mess.

Lucas decided that it was time for the next meal. It was close to supper time, so he asked Clair what she wanted for dinner.

He was gratified by a giggle from Clair who was always reminded not to use too much syrup.

She chose pancakes.

Lucas found a camping cook stove and prepared some pancakes. He opened a can of spam to act as the sausage. The syrup and hot pancakes seemed to cheer Clair up.

Lady eagerly ate a small piece of pancake, a piece of spam and licked the syrup off the paper plates.

Lucas gave Clair a bottle of water. He poured a little out for Lady.

Lucas let Clair know that he was going to go to check on old man Dan. He asked Clair if she would be OK by herself until he got back.

He would have preferred to take her along with him, but the rain continued to fall in sheets. She would be much safer in the shelter.

He put the bed back in order and straightened out the bed so that Clair could sleep on a level bed.

He found a toy box Evelyn had prepared and brought it to the end of the bed. There was an old cloth doll inside. "Does she have a name? Why don't you take care of her while I'm gone? She's probably scared too," Lucas said quietly.

"Her name is Mable. How long will you be gone? Uncle Lucas," Clair asked quietly.

He promised to be back before the lamp ran out of fuel but that she should go to bed and get a good night of sleep.

He made sure the lantern was full of fuel and pumped up. He set it as low as he could.

"It will take me most of the night.

See the clock on the post? I am going to mark when I should be back," Lucas said, and he took one of the markers from the coloring set and marked the nine. He hoped to be back hours before, but he did not want to take a chance in scaring Clair.

Lucas instructed Clair to stay in the safe shelter. He gave her a hug and a kiss on the forehead and whispered that she was safe.

Once again, he made sure he had what he thought he might need in his backpack. He then put on his poncho and stepped back out into the rain.

He set out in the rain and headed along the ridge toward Dan's place. He continued to thank his walking stick for its support. He was about halfway there when he literally ran into a train wreck. It took him a few minutes to figure out what the barrier looming over him was. A pile of rail cars obstructed the trail ahead.

He carefully picked his way through and around the cars. Then he continued up the trail toward Dan's place. He didn't know what to make of the train wreck. It was beyond what he could comprehend. He decided for the time he would just accept it and go on.

Dan's place was a repeat of what he had found at Jim and Evelyn's place. He knew he was in the right clearing. It was empty and the pouring rain made it impossible to see anything clearly.

He made his way back to the cured meat storage niche in the cliff. This was similar to Jim's and Evelyn's storm cellar but significantly smaller. Inside Lucas found a tumult of cured meats and sausages, a small old cast iron stove and some ancient pots and pans.

Lucas had come to realize that survival was becoming the next challenge. The treasure in this cave for Lucas was the large amount of cured meats. This cache of meats along with the food in Jim and Evelyn's shelter meant that he and Clair had more than enough to carry them through almost two entire years.

The total devastation of three homes, the train wreck on the mountain side and the continuing hard rain indicated some unimagined catastrophe.

Lucas could not make any sense of it. The Event was so far a nature disaster mystery. He let his mid absorb the situation, but he did not know how to process what was being absorbed.

He knew he was in a state of shock because he was not trying to put a rational spin to his now alien surrounding. He was accepting it and taking stock in the situation he found himself and now Clair in.

Once again, he realized how relieved he was to have found Clair.

He decided that he would be practical. He put a smoked ham in his backpack. He would come back later and get the rest.

He needed to get back to Clair.

He was getting ready to leave when he heard whining coming from across the clearing.

He located the source of the whining. A young spotted hound still attached to a chain lay in the rain. The dog had a stick that had gone all the way through his leg.

Lucas unhooked the chain from the dog's collar and carried him into the meat locker. He looked at the wound and knew he would have to remove the stick.

"Ok boy, this is going to hurt. Please don't bite me when I pull out the stick," Lucas said quietly as he stroked the hound on his snout and between his ears.

He looked at how the stick was situated and decided a quick pull outward would be the best way. He was still worried about getting bitten, so he strapped the hound to the board he had laid him on. The strap went across the hound's front quarter.

Lucas put his left hand flat on the hind quarter with his thumb on one side of the stick and his fingers on the other side. He firmly grasped the stick with his right hand and swiftly pulled the stick out.

There was almost no blood.

"Well, this is good. Let me get some stuff from my medical kit and bandage this wound," Lucas spoke to the hound.

The dog was amazingly docile.

"Well, I wonder what your story would be if you could talk," Lucas said as he stroked the young hound along his neck.

Lucas cut a piece of smoked ham and gave it to the young dog. It was clear he was very hungry.

Lucas cut a piece of meat for himself.

"You will have to walk back on your own. I will tie your leash to my belt so we won't get separated," Lucas talked to the dog as if he would understand.

Lucas looked out of the small cave. There seemed to be no letup in the rain.

It was time to go back to Clair. He stood up and led the dog out into the rain.

Lucas led the way down the trail and the hound limped eagerly behind him. It was clear he did not want to be left behind.

Once again, the train blocked his way.

Lucas stopped to examine the train wreck. He now began to wonder if there might be anyone alive in all the wreckage. There was no way he could navigate safely through all the rubble that seemed to be about.

The rain made it impossible to see anything clearly.

He was just getting ready to move on when a banging noise caught his attention.

He had no way of knowing that the person doing the banging would be the soul mate that he had been wishing for. Her arrival was just not what he had expected.

Chapter 13: Anna, on the Trail

Anna came to. It was still raining. She ate her fourth and last sandwich. She was confused and in a daze. Slowly she recalled where she was. She was unsure of the time but by her sandwich clock she must have been in the wreck for at least two days.

She had been on her way back home to Sao Paulo after visiting her friend in Rio. She had taken the early Sunday morning train out of Rio. Once the train got underway, she had stopped at the lounge car for a breakfast snack. Just after sitting down with a cup of coffee and her snack, as she took her first bite the world went crazy. She watched as the people in the car went floating into the air. Her reaction was to pull herself under the round table where she was sitting. She wrapped her arms tightly around the center leg. She watched as the couple in front of her hit the ceiling. She hit her head on the bottom of the table. That was the last thing she could remember.

She woke up under the table and she had a broken leg. After finally getting up on the bench seat she was able to set the broken bone by wedging her foot under a heavy bar and pushing herself up the bench. She had passed out with the pain.

There was now enough light to let her see the dining car was in total ruin. The area behind the counter was smashed in. Anyone back there would have been crushed. The two other passengers, in the car with her, had not moved during the several times she was awake. She was sure they were dead.

She looked for a way out but realized she could not get out the windows. They had been crushed and they were no more than twelve-centimeter slits. In a way she was lucky they were so small. Most of the rain coming down in a torrent was kept out.

She found her cell phone, but it was useless. She dialed work, friends, and her parents. There were no answers to any of her calls. The day passed slowly. No one came.

She was a member on her hospital rescue squad. She knew they would be trying their best to find survivors. She decided to swing a steel rod back and forth along the window opening. She hoped this noise and motion would attract attention.

She pulled out her Kindle from her purse and selected a story to read. She figured she might as well relax and hope the rescuers would hear the rod, she was absent mindedly pushing back and forth. She wondered what someone watching her would think of her actions

Through the pouring rain Lucas could just barely hear a sliding sound. He took out his flashlight and tried to get a better view of the train wreck.

Lucas wondered if someone was trying to make themselves noticed or whether it was just the rain rattling some loose piece of metal.

He began to call out.

Anna heard what she thought was someone calling. She found her penlight and reached up to the window and turned it on and off.

Lucas was slowly turning in the pouring rain trying to get his bearings when he saw the tiny flicker of light. He moved carefully toward the barely visible flicker. He was not really sure if it was real.

"Hello, can you hear me," Lucas shouted through the rain.

Anna was surprised to hear English.

Anna wondered where this rescuer had come from.

She was so happy to hear the voice. She responded in Portuguese and then quickly repeated in English.

"Yes, I can hear you. I am trapped in this dining car," Anna called out.

She was saved! She would survive. Tears were running down her cheek.

Lucas took in the damaged rail car. He felt as much as saw the condition of the car. The rain made it impossible to see the whole car at once. He found the door and steps of the car. The steps were gone and now there was a hole a person could get through. The car must have fallen on its top and then rolled back upright. There was just enough room for a person to crawl out.

"Can you get to the lower end of the car? There seems to be an opening through which you can crawl," Lucas called out.

"I am not sure I can do it by myself. My leg is broken," Anna replied.

She wondered what kind of rescue team this could be. They were not very capable or effective. Where was their gear?

Lucas shouted to the person that he would be in to help her in a moment.

He found a piece of the train that he flipped up at an angle and created a temporary shelter. He took off his backpack and rain gear and stacked them out of the rain. He tied the dog to a bar that was under the lean-to.

"You stay here and guard this stuff," Lucas said as he patted the dog on the head.

Lucas was soaked by the time he managed to crawl into what was left of the rail car. The car was close to a forty-five-degree angle to the level.

He crawled through the water to where a young lady was laying in the V of the lounge bench. She had managed to remain dry.

Do think you can crawl out," Lucas asked.

"Where is the flat board? Where are your helpers," Anna asked. She wondered what kind of rescue team she had run into.

Lucas introduced himself and asked her name. He could see that she was stressed and exhausted.

He told her he was not part of a rescue team and that he was alone.

"We either do this together or you're going to have to stay," Lucas replied.

"I am Anna," she replied.

Anna thought for a moment.

"OK, help me splint my leg. I need two straight pieces of wood or steel to go up both sides of my leg. Then you will have to bind my leg to those splints," Anna instructed.

"I have a rescuer that needs instruction. What is next," Anna thought to herself.

Lucas located two pieces of metal trim he thought might have been part of the window frame. He then ripped the vinyl strips about an inch wide from the bench seat and carefully bound Anna's leg. He knew it must have been painful because several times she cried out but encourage him to continue.

Finally, the splints were tied in place.

"Let me slide myself down to the opening. You go out ahead of me and guide my legs out," Anna instructed.

She had decided she would be in charge of the rescue. She would later complain to the Rail Authority.

Lucas carefully guided Anna's legs out through the opening.

When they were clear of the rail car, he pulled her into his chest and picked her up in a hug like carry.

He slowly maneuvered through the rain. He noted she was not dressed for winter weather.

He had three layers of clothes on and his rain gear and had still been cold. How she had survived in the car was a mystery.

He carried Anna to his makeshift lean too.

"Are you one of the passengers," Anna asked as she realized the magnitude of the accident.

"No, I live nearby," Lucas replied.

He was looking around for the makings of a modern-day travois. He would need to pull Anna back to the shelter where Clair was waiting. He was now glad he had put all the extra time on the clock. He knew Clair would be watching it.

At the moment Lucas was glad the drumming of the rain on the tin of the lean-to made it almost impossible to talk.

Anna was taking in what she could of the wreck, but she was again feeling faint. She was totally confused and disoriented. The amount of water and the noise of the rain were overwhelming. She closed her eyes and tried to relax against the pain coursing up her leg.

Lucas found what appeared to be the flexible membrane section that served to seal the openings between two rail cars. It had a heavy rod on each side and the canvas connected the two.

He was able to make minor modifications with his knife to modify the carrying area. He pulled the travois under the lean-to.

He noticed Anna was either sleeping or had passed out. It would be a rough ride back to the storage shed and Clair and she might as well be asleep.

He placed Anna on the travois. Then he secured her so she would not slide off.

Next, he put the dog on the travois next to Anna and covered them both with his rain poncho.

He hoped they would warm each other during the ride back to the shelter.

Lucas looked once more at the wreckage and wondered if there might be other survivors. He had noticed the two dead bodies in the car Anna had occupied.

There was no time for him to search and there was no way that in the continuing rain he could do it without risking his life and now potentially risking two other lives.

Chapter 14: Muri, John, and the Tortoise.

Muri was aware that almost two days had passed. They had completed making their rope and were anxious to get back to the village.

Their lantern had run out of fuel, and they spent their time in almost total darkness. They had eaten almost all of their catfish and the rain never stopped. It seemed to have gotten a little less intense, but it still fell heavily.

Muri voiced his worry about their families and suggested they try and get down out of the cave.

"I think we need to take a chance and move out of our cave. Our families will be worried, and they may need our help," Muir said as he once again took the long stick and felt along the surface below the cave opening.

There seemed to be some foot holds that would allow climbing down.

"How are we both going to go down," John asked.

"We will tie the rope to this stick. We can put the stick across the opening. Once we reach the bottom, we can jog the stick to one side and pull it and the rope down to us," Muri said as he showed how it could be accomplished.

He once again took the long stick and felt along the surface below the cave opening.

"All right, I am the lightest so I should go first," John replied.

Muri agreed. He would hold the rope while John climbed down. They had agreed that they would only take their knife and the rope.

John slowly backed out of the cave. The rain immediately pulled at him and caused him alarm. He was good at climbing and could scale almost any cliff by hand without the need of a rope, but the rain made it impossible to see. He felt along with his feet and was glad to feel the ridges and holes in the rock face. He slowly made his way down. He got to the end of the rope and still he was not at the bottom.

"I am going to let go and jump down the rest of the way," John shouted up to Muri.

There was no answer. It was impossible to hear through the torrent of rain.

As soon as the rope went loose Muri knew either John had made it to the bottom, or he had fallen. He hurriedly backed himself out of the cave and started down the cliff.

He came to the end of the rope and realized he had not made it to the bottom.

He wondered what John had done. He knew John probably jumped.

Muri was not so keen to do the same but there seemed to be no alternative. He was about to let go of the rope when suddenly a set of arms went around his calves. He almost fell, and then he realized it was John.

John was laughing hysterically.

Muri flicked the rope to the left.

The rope stick and he collapsed on top of John.

When John let go of the rope, he prepared for a long fall. But he was only four feet off the ground. He almost hurt himself because he was not ready to land so soon. Then he realized Muri would do the same and possible hurt himself. He stood up but got disoriented. He finally touched the cliff and almost at the same time saw Muri's legs.

John was a little hysterical. The rain was so heavy it was hard to breathe and almost impossible to see.

Muri asked what John thought was so funny.

"It's either this or I will cry. Let's see if we can find the path leading to the top," John shouted through the rain.

Muri led the way along the cliff face toward the trail. It was impossible to see anything clearly. He almost missed the trail but the old rope leading upward hit him in the side of the head.

This time it was his turn to laugh. He was sure anyone watching would have thought both of them a little crazy. And he realized that they would have been right.

He shouted at John to be careful on the way up.

Going up was easier than Muri anticipated. The water had washed away all the loose stones and other debris.

Once at the top Muri and John stopped as they tried to get their bearings. The path was ancient and well-worn but getting home in the torrent of rain would take all their skill at tracking and following sign. To keep to the trail, they would literally need to crawl on their hands and knees and feel their way along.

It turned out that the most ancient part of the trail that was worn into the stone remained but the parts of the trail that had been made of dirt were gone.

Muri almost jumped up and ran when he came face to face with a huge turtle. It was upside down and struggling to right itself.

When he suddenly backed up John hit him on his butt with his head.

"Hey, what's the matter," John said both startled and a little angry. The rain was driving him crazy.

Muri pulled him up next to him and pointed at the huge upside-down turtle. It probably weighed as much as the two of them together.

Muri stood up and went to one side of the turtle. He positioned John next to him. It took them three tries as they rocked the turtle back and forth to put it on its feet. The turtle then slowly lumbered away from them.

"You know we could regret not killing it to eat," John said.

"Yes, I thought of that. Let's hope we don't," Muri said as he got back on his hands and knees and continued to navigate along the trail.

The next strange thing they found on the trail was a giant conch shell.

"It looks as if the ocean has dumped its contents here. Look over there, is that an octopus," John asked?

The crab Muri held up was dead, but it appeared rather fresh. He took out his knife and cut off the two large claws. He and John took turns using the knife to dig out the meat as they sat close together in the pouring rain. They were hungry enough to enjoy the raw crab.

Once they had their fill, they continued their crawl back to the village.

Finally, they found themselves at the village center stone. This was the pointed projection of a stone coming up from the earth. The village leaders believed it was part of the bed rock. It held mystical powers and was the gathering place and the place of worship.

John and Muri examined the stone projection carefully. It was their village center stone. It had writing on it. The situation began to coalesce. Something was very wrong. The sitting stones located around the center stone and all other artifacts were missing.

Muri held their rope and John crawled in a circle around the stone; nothing, no houses, no village. There were no buildings anywhere.

What could possibly have happened?

"Let's see if the meeting house is still there," John shouted to Muri. The meeting house was made of stone and mortar. It was the most substantial structure in the village.

"OK, let's crawl to it," Muri shouted back.

As they crawled toward the house, they ran into a structure so huge and so out of place they did not know what it was.

Muri actually hit his head on the structure and after feeling around, he shouted through the rain," I think it's a truck or cargo container."

Together they worked their way around to the end and figured out how to open it. The container was full. They move some of the boxes out into the rain and then crawled in. They had to get out of the rain. They threw out enough of the goods inside to create a space large enough to lay down.

They huddled together to stay warm and fell asleep.

142

Chapter 15: Cualli, Tosi and Dolphins

Cualli finally got his fire going in the fire ring Tosi had made toward the back corner of the overhang.

They kept the fire small, but it put out enough heat to warm them.

A few of the coconuts in the pile of debris held promise as a source of something to eat. It was clear they would need to find more food if they were to survive.

Cualli announced that he was going to explore their surroundings. Neither of them had any idea where they were.

There seemed to be no letup, a solid sheet of water was falling from the sky.

Cualli decided he should look for some source of food. He suggested Tosi stay and continue to organize their shelter.

She had wanted to go along but Cualli pointedly told her she needed to recover some more, and she needed more clothes to keep her warm.

Cualli went out and in the opposite direction from where they had come. He soon reached sand. He went to the left and hit water. He went to the right and again hit water, but he realized there were no waves. He went in a zigzag back and forth and soon realized he was on an atoll island or on a long peninsula with water at each side. Then he met another stranded porpoise. This one was a lot smaller than the first one he and Tosi had rescued.

"Well, my friend, let's see if I can pull you down to the lagoon," Cualli said as he slowly pulled the porpoise by the tale into the clam water.

Cualli tried to remember which way he and Tosi had pulled the other porpoise. The water on this side was calm so he thought it was the same side.

Cualli was not sure whether he should continue on. A few moments later he fell over the body of a dead calf. The calf was probably less than a year old. He knew that he had to get the calf back to the shelter.

The calf was heavier than he thought and presented a challenge. The rain was an additional challenge in getting it back to the shelter.

Cualli knew he and Tosi would need to cook the meat or dry it. It would also provide them with material to make some sort of clothing.

Cualli chuckled as he thought about what each of them was wearing. They certainly did not have on their survival gear. He was in shorts sporting a loin cloth and Tosi was in a white bikini. They had lost the long white wrap that had saved their lives.

It took more than an hour to slowly drag the calf back. He was glad it wasn't any older.

Tosi came to help him as he pulled the dead animal into the dry of the overhang.

"Did you find anything we could use as a knife," Cualli asked Tosi.

"The only hard object I found is a large conch shell," Tosi replied.

"If we can create a blade from the conch, we may be able to use the handle of my fake sacrificial knife to make a real knife," Cualli said as he looked at the conch and examined the fake knife handle.

He looked at the handle in surprise when he realized that somehow it had stayed in the belt line of his shorts.

It was getting noticeably cooler. Cualli did not know if he was just experiencing hypothermia from essentially walking in the rain with no clothes, but it really did not matter. He looked around and was glad to see a significant supply of stones the size of basket balls.

Cualli suggested they built a wall and create a room in the back corner of the shelter. It was the high spot in the overhand and seemed to have remained dry.

Cualli and Tosi spent the next few hours building the walls for their shelter. They chased out two crabs from the pile of debris. They were happy to see them scurry away.

"Multiply and be fruitful," Tosi called out after them as they disappeared out into the rain.

Tosi used some of the dry grasses and old palm leaves she had taken from the corner and stuffed them between the stones.

It was a three-sided shelter with the small fire immediately in front of the entrance.

Tosi declared it home and suitable for them to sleep in.

The two then worked for several hours to make a conch shell knife with a ceremonial sacrifice handle.

Tosi did a superb job of creating a sharp cutting edge by carefully chipping a large piece of conch shell into a blade like implement.

Cualli was able to secure the conch blade into the sacrificial handle to create a very effective knife.

Cualli said a prayer of thanks for the knife. He then cut off the calf's tongue and put it on a stick so it could get roasted.

Tosi took a stick, skewered tongue, and held it over the small fire. Cualli then began to skin the calf. He had only watched as his uncle and father butchered cows. He remembered how they cut down the inside of each leg and then carefully pulled and lightly cut the skin off the flesh. They always lifted the cow by the back legs up off the ground. He knew he would have to do his skinning differently. He rolled the calf first one way and loosened the skin to the middle of the back and then rolled it the other way.

Cualli was glad that it was a calf and not a fully grown cow or bull He was successful in getting the hide off without putting any holes in it. He now faced the task of gutting the cow. This and disposing of the un-useable parts would be the worst part of the butchering.

"Hey, take a break and get over here and eat your fill of tongue," Tosi called out.

She had peeled the skin off the tongue as she grilled it over the fire.

She knew she was really hungry because she was willing to overcome a lifelong phobia against eating weird parts of animals. The smell of the cooking meat was making her mouth water.

The rain turned out to be a help in processing the entrails. Cualli wanted to save everything possible. The intestines would make great thread and might serve as fishing line. The hide would provide material for clothes. The bones would yield sewing needles, fishhooks, and bone handles for tools. Every part of this animal would be used to ensure their survival.

He was now thinking of survival and the fact there might be no rescue.

"You know it is getting colder. I am going to scrape the hide and begin to get it ready to make some clothes," Tosi said as she pulled the hide back toward their new room.

"I'm going to make a small fire in one corner of the room. It will never be more than two handfuls in size, but it should take the chill out of the air," Cualli said as he brought the coals from the first fire back into the room.

Tosi used the hide to close the door and she and Cualli reclined on a pile of dry seaweed she had rescued from the pile of debris.

"Debris, more like treasure," Tosi thought as she fell asleep in Cualli's arms.

Chapter 16: Clair, Anna, Lady, and the Tramp

Clair had eaten her snack. She had played with her doll. She had gone to the door and called out for Mommy and Daddy. The rain was heavy and dark. She looked at the clock. The little hand still had a long way to go to get to the mark Uncle Lucas had put on the clock.

Clair ate the pancakes and syrup Uncle Lucas left for her. He had also left a candy bar. She saved that to just before she decided to take a nap. She crawled under the blanket and fell asleep with the bar only half eaten.

Lady helped her by eating the rest and then curled up next to her.

Lucas moved along the trail as quickly as he could, but the going was slow. He balanced speed with staying on the trail and he worked hard to keep the travois from tipping over.

He was on the ridge hiking trail and there were some very narrow points.

The fact that the trail seemed to be cleared of all loose rocks and limbs made the going easier. His walking stick was now on the travois next to Anna.

The intense rain kept him from seeing any of the surrounding, but he knew if he could see it, it would be an alien sight. Things seemed very different.

He hoped Clair would be OK. He had left her with some food to eat and there was plenty of food in the shelter. He just needed to get back and get back soon. He was now beginning to worry about his condition. He was totally soaked, and the weather seemed to be getting colder.

Lucas almost walked by the shelter. Then he heard Lady barking. He instinctively turned and walked toward the sound. Lady had just earned her life-long keep. She had kept him from walking past the shelter.

He knew he was on his last ounce of energy. He managed to open the door and pull the travois into the room.

The dog on the travois crawled out wagging his tail.

"Oh, you brought Tramp," Clair said excitedly.

Clair's voice gave Lucas a surge of energy. He walked over to the pantry and opened a can of spam and a box of hard dark crackers. He felt better after a couple of bites. He looked at the clock. It was exactly the time he had promised Clair and at least three hours longer than he had planned. He ate a few more bites of food and then decided he wanted to get into dry clothes.

Clair lifted the raincoat and looked under it.

"Oh, who is this," Clair said touching Anna's cheek?

"Her name is Anna. She has a broken leg. I found her on the trail when I went to Old Dan's place. I found Tramp on a chain at Dan's.

Well, I brought Tramp and sleeping beauty home together.

Lucas went over to the bed. He pulled back the cover and arranged the pillows. He went over to where Anna was laying and untied the raincoat.

He examined Anna in the lantern light.

He was surprised by her beauty. Even in her battered condition she was gorgeous. He got a washcloth and used a bottle of water to wet it. He realized Anna had a high fever. He took off all her wet clothes dried her off and carried her over to the bed. He found some of Evelyn's old flannel night clothes and put the top on Anna.

He then checked her leg. He was startled at the gash where the bone had come out. The bone felt like it had been properly set. He used some peroxide to clean out the wound.

Then using some sutures from the first aid kit, he carefully made a couple of internal stitches. These pulled the flesh back together.

Next, he closed the skin with a mattress stitch that pulled the skin together in a fine straight line. Only the ends of the sutures were visible. These would need to be pulled out in a few days. He hoped he had done an adequate repair job. He knew that no one else was available to do what he had just done.

He had learned about stitching up cuts like this from his veterinarian friend Bob. He was sure Bob would have approved of the stitching he had just completed. Of course, Bob would have been stitching on a dog.

He was also glad that that his patient had passed out.

"I wonder what Anna is going to think," Lucas thought as he finished dressing her and covering her with a blanket.

He looked through the boxes of clothes meant for Jim and found some that would fit him. He changed out of his wet clothes and then he prepared something for all of them to eat.

He put chicken broth in a pot and cut some vegetables into it. He cut a piece of meat from the ham hock he had brought from Old Dan's place and then cut it into small chunks. Once he had the soup cooked, he brought a bowl over to the bed. He got Anna to swallow three aspirin and then slowly spooned the broth into her mouth. She was not fully awake but seemed able to swallow the broth from the soup. He was able to get at least a cup of soup into her.

During this entire time Clair was sitting on the floor between Lady and the hound he had brought back. Clair had immediately named him Tramp.

It was clear she had been hungry as well as she busily ate her soup. She periodically gave a chunk of meat to Lady and the Tramp.

"Thank you for bringing Tramp for Lady. Do you think you will be able to find Mommy and Daddy," Clair asked quietly?

Lucas could see the beginning of tears in Clair's eyes. Somehow Clair knew something bad had happened.

"Sweetheart, I am not sure where to look for your Mommy or Daddy. I will look for them but until I find them, I will take care of you," Lucas said with tears in his eyes.

He walked over to Clair and picked her up and gave her a hug.

"You know, I love you," Lucas said to her

"I know," Clair said quietly as she hugged him back.

Lucas felt better after he had eaten but he was still exhausted. There was only the queen size bed in the shelter.

After feeding the two dogs and cleaning up the shelter Lucas tucked a folded blanket along the outer edge of the bed on Anna's side. He did not want her to roll out on the floor.

Lucas put Clair in the middle with Lady at her feet and climbed in on the opposite side of where Anna was laying.

Tramp lay below him on the floor.

It was great to be dry and once he blew out the lantern he was in deep sleep.

Anna woke to a quiet, dark room. She was in a warm comfortable bed. Her leg ached and she remembered being rescued by some American. She felt to her left and was surprised to feel a little body next to her. She reached over and felt a larger adult body beyond. She looked carefully around. She was not in a hospital and not in someone's home. It seemed to be an old shed. She was disoriented. Nothing was making sense.

A warm tongue startled her, and she almost let out a yelp. She smiled to herself. It was a dog. He lay beside her on the bed. No wonder she felt so toasty. She stroked the dog behind his ears. This was so strange. Then she noticed it was still raining hard. She had never experienced so much rain for so long. The air was frosty. She pulled the blanket up to her chin. She also realized she was in bed with a totally different set of clothes.

"I am not sure where I am and with who, but I am comfortable for the first time since leaving Rio," Anna thought to herself.

She decided to go back to sleep.

Clair was quietly watching Anna. She put her hand on Anna's cheek. Anna was just getting ready to go back to sleep.

"I'm Clair," she said in a whisper.

"I'm Anna," Anna replied. She had no idea who this young girl might be. Things just kept getting stranger.

"You're Anna, I'm Clair," Clair said and moved closer to Anna.

"I wonder when we were introduced," Anna thought putting her arm around the small figure. Almost immediately she fell asleep.

Lady came over and found a spot on the bed near Clair's feet and curled up and fell asleep.

Lucas slept on peacefully through the night as the rain continued in a deluge.

Chapter 17: Homestead and Winter

Lucas awoke when Clair crawled over him. She needed to potty. Lucas thought about this situation and knew he had to create an outdoor area to serve as the latrine.

He needed something immediately to handle the current situation.

Lucas got up and went to the door. The rain had not let up.

He turned back into the room. He was thinking about the biblical story of Noah and the forty days and forty nights of rain.

"OK, I am going to put this big pot in the corner and put a curtain around it. Don't fall into the pot," he instructed Clair.

He would probably take off all his clothes and go out in the rain when it came his turn. It would be a shower as well.

When he turned back to the bed, he saw Anna quietly looking around.

"Good morning. How do you feel," he asked?

"I feel good actually, but I am really confused," Anna said as she pulled herself into a sitting position and arranged her pillow behind her.

"Are you hungry," Lucas asked. "I am getting ready to fix some breakfast.

I know I can do pancakes with smoked ham but beyond that I don't have a clue," he volunteered

Pancakes and ham will be fine. Do you have any coffee," Anna asked?

"Oh, and by the way where are my clothes," she continued.

The flannel night clothes felt fine, but she was thinking about getting dressed so she could get up.

"I'm not sure your clothes are dry yet. I rinsed them off in the rain last night. Let me see if Evelyn has any clothes that might fit you. She is taller than you but there will probably be some sweats that will do," Lucas said as he rummaged through the clothes box.

He found a matching blue sweat pant and jacket.

"Here we are, this should keep you warm," Lucas said bringing the clothes over to Anna.

"How does your leg feel," Lucas continued as he lifted the blanket.

He pulled up the pajama pant leg to look at the wound.

Ann was surprised to see her leg cleaned and stitched. A nylon stocking had been pulled on. There were two clean wooden splints tied to each side. A slit in the stocking left the wound open and exposed.

"Did you do the stitching," Anna inquired. She was impressed by the clean, neat work. Once healed there would almost be no scar.

"Well, Clair wanted to do the stitching, but I told her next time," Lucas joked.

"The three internal stitches will need to be pulled out later. I left the ends sticking out," Lucas went on and lightly flicked the filaments sticking through the skin.

"Are you a doctor," Anna asked?

"No, by trade I am an architect. I grew up just down the trail on the family homestead. It was not exactly a farm, but we raised rabbits, chickens, once in a while a pig, goat, or lamb," Lucas replied.

"I am a medical surgeon, and I am currently a resident at a local hospital. Your work on my leg would qualify you as a top doctor," Anna congratulated Lucas.

"Well, thanks but everything I learned was from my animal veterinarian friend down in Buchanan. I guess it works on people too," Lucas said with a grin.

"Where am I," Anna finally dared to ask.

"You are up on a mountain above the town of Buchanan, Virginia. Where did you think you might be," Lucas asked?

"I boarded the train in Rio de Janeiro and was on the way to Sao Paulo," Anna replied quietly.

Something major that she did not comprehend had happened.

"Well, I can confirm, I took you off a train crash located up the ridge trail. It seems to have been dropped there from the sky," Lucas said bringing a plate of pancakes with ham and a cup of coffee to the bed.

The magnitude of the Event was beginning to sink in. He did not yet understand what had happened but the fact that a train traveling between Rio and Sao Paulo would end up on a mountain top above Buchanan was indeed wildly impossible.

"I'm done," Clair announce as she came out from behind the blanket in the corner.

Lucas carefully took the pot and set it outside of the door. He hoped the rain would wash it out and make it ready for the next use.

He came back and went to the plate with the pancakes and prepared one for Clair.

"I returned to the homestead after too much partying and by old habit I went to my hiding cave to sleep it off. When I got up yesterday or whenever it was, I was battered and bruised as if I had been in a fight. I finally ventured out into the rain to go to my house, but it was gone.

After recovering I came up to see if I could help Evelyn, John, and Clair. Clair's house was gone when I got here. I found Clair and then set out to check on Dan. His house was gone when I got there. The train is between here and Old Dan's place," Lucas recounted.

"The "Event" people have been talking about really happened. I am not sure what happened but, on this mountain, it has been devastating," Lucas replied.

"There are three of us here. If I collect the food, I know is up at Old Dan's place and add it to this supply and the supply I have back at my place, we have enough to survive the winter and well into the following year.

But we also have to keep warm and dry. I would like to do that at my place. There we will have more room and we will have two places. The cave and the cool room," Lucas shared.

Lucas had already started the planning of how he would get everyone to the cool room at his place.

"What can I do to help," Anna asked.

She knew it would be a few more days before she could get up and about. Even then she would be limited in what she could do until her leg healed.

"Actually, playing and taking care of Clair will be a big help. I will be moving everything I can to my homestead. I want to do that immediately. If this rain turns to snow, we will be buried by it. We need the best shelter we can devise.

In the following week, Lucas only came back to the shelter to eat and sleep. The rain continued unabated. He moved all the food, old tools, and the old pot-bellied stove from Old Dan's place to his cave.

Lucas found bodies in almost every rail car, but he said nothing to Anna or Clair about them. It turned out there was a fair amount of food and drink on the train. This he took straight to the cool room at his homestead.

The landing impact shattered or blew apart some of the rail cars. Lucas stacked the loose panels from these cars aside. He envisioned using them to build a house later in the spring.

He recovered several toolboxes. He also located a fuel tank and moved about one hundred gallons of fuel and put it in a barrel just outside of the cool room.

He brought suitcases back to the shelter. Anna and Clair rummaged through the luggage and separated out clothes and items they thought would be immediately useful. Clair liked opening the suitcases to see what was inside. Anna knew the owners were most likely dead somewhere on the train but said nothing.

Anna's survival was a miracle. Her car must have come down upside down and hit the car just uphill of it. It crushed that car and itself and then rolled off downhill to land on a forty-five-degree angle across the trail. The car it landed on was crushed to about a two-foot height. The dining car fared better only because the counters and tables were about four foot high.

Two cars were almost totally intact and undamaged except the glass was shattered. Overall, there were few people on board. This was probably due to the fact that it was an early Sunday morning run.

At the end of the week Lucas began moving the things from Evelyn's and Jim's shelter to his place. He moved everything he could in large waterproof back packs. The rain never let up for the entire time. If there had been any survivors in Buchanan the entire town would by now have been swept away down the river.

"I can't move the bed. The mattress would get soaked. We will need to wait until the rain stops," Lucas said as he came back from taking the last load he planned to move to his homestead.

He was leaving some food, clothes, and blankets in the shelter for emergency situations.

He found a set of crutches on the train and had adjusted them to fit Anna.

"There is also no way of getting you there totally dry. I have given up in either being dry or totally warm and comfortable. It's getting progressively colder and soon it will be snowing. I was hoping the rain would stop before it got cold enough to snow.

"It's time to take you and Clair to the homestead," Lucas announced.

"Here is your coach," Lucas proudly declared as he pulled in a modified baby carriage. He had tested his coach by pulling almost three hundred pounds of materials and tools between the shelter and the home stead.

"You're kidding," Ann said as she looked skeptically at the modified carriage.

"Nope; I have tested it and it is ready for you and Clair." The dogs will have to walk. I will pull you along the trail.

"Sit down and put Clair on your good side. You will be inside a plastic covering. If you can keep all the edges tucked in, you might even get there in a dry condition. However, getting there dry, is not guaranteed," Lucas said as he helped Anna sit down.

"Ooh! A buggy ride," Clair said excitedly.

The weather turned as Lucas pulled the buggy along the trail to the homestead. The rain began to be more like slush. He increased his pace. He did not relish getting caught in a blizzard. It was already a huge challenge navigating the trail in the heavy rain.

He had planted markers about every thirty feet along the trail. Now he was almost running by them. The falling rain was freezing on the ground. He was getting coated in a layer of ice. The covering over Anna and Clair was beginning to sag under the weight of the slush.

Clair whispered excitedly and giggled as the buggy bumped along the trail. Anna talked quietly back but she was aware it was getting markedly colder, and the covering was getting heavy with ice. She kept slapping at the cover to make the ice fall off. She was worried and concerned they would not make it.

As he ran by the garden area the rain turned to a full-blown blizzard. Now Lucas was running through a solid wall of falling snow.

"Come on Lady, Come on Tramp," Lucas shouted as he trotted along. Both dogs were struggling to keep up.

Lucas almost ran into the rock wall. He was so glad to have made it. He located the door and pulled the carriage over to it.

"My queen and princess, you have arrived at your castle," Lucas said as he helped Clair and Anna into the cool room. He had moved the freezer outside to make more room inside.

"That was close wasn't it," Anna said as he helped her in.

"Yes, I am not sure how much snow we will have but I think it will set a record if it continues as long as the rain did," Lucas quietly replied.

Clair had found the living area and was sitting on the rug with Lady and Tramp.

Anna went over to a rocking chair and sat down. The light was dim, but she could see that the long cool room had been organized to have a sleeping area on one end, a cooking area by the entrance and a storage area at the far end.

By this time, she was aware of Lucas's penchant for organizing his environment and she was sure he had located a latrine somewhere outside.

Lucas was changing out of his wet clothes behind a changing screen.

Anna took note that Lucas had made sure each of them could have privacy when changing clothes.

Chapter 18: Sunlight

Lucas had carefully established a calendar that he kept in their sitting area. Anna had participated in setting it up as well. He was certain it had a one-or-two-day accuracy. There were thirty-three R's signifying rain marked on the calendar.

He was now putting the twentieth S on the calendar to signify snow.

It was now February sixth on his calendar.

The temperature had remained in the low twenties for the entire twenty days. Lucas was resigned to it remaining bitterly cold.

The only thing saving them from the large amount of snow was the high wind. It constantly swept through the area in front of the cool room and cleared much of the snow away.

Lucas was constantly clearing away the snow that swept up against the cool room area.

Lucas was worried as the diesel fuel he had retrieved from the train slowly ran down. He had to keep the old stove he had from Dan's place burning.

In the continuing blizzard he had no way of getting back to the train for more fuel.

The cool room had one feature that was constant. Summer or winter the room always stayed at about forty degrees. The only really warm area was immediately around the stove. Lucas put up some curtains to create a small warm area. The rest of the room stayed at its normal temperature.

He knew he could stretch the fuel to last well into early summer. He just wasn't sure there would be a summer.

Lucas marked his twenty-eighth S on the calendar. It was now mid-February and the snows had not abated. The snow was as thick as the rain had been. It was impossible to go out any distance from the cool room. Lucas had made a path to the hillside where he was currently dumping waste. He had pounded in long rods and put a rope guide on the poles. He had another path out to gather clean snow to melt for water. He was determined save as much of the bottled water as possible. It was used only for cooking.

Each evening Lucas would bring out his old guitar and the three would sing the songs they could remember. Anna had a great voice and carried Lucas through the songs. She coached Clair and the two would practice singing throughout the day.

Lucas kept busy preparing his seeds. He had some starter containers in the corner but would only be able to use them if he could find enough soil to fill them.

He inventoried his tools. He had one gas powered electric generator that he had stored in the cave. He moved all the power tools into storage with the generator. He knew of another electric generator on the train but had left it behind. The generator might be useful in the future but for now he needed to conserve fuel.

He knew the train would also be the source of fuel but for now he would stick to his lanterns.

His lanterns were much more efficient, and they also provided a fair amount of heat.

The only known bed in the region was back in Jim's and Evelyn's shelter. There was no way to transport it undamaged to the cool room. The three slept together on a raised wooden platform made with a four by eight-foot piece of plywood Lucas had retrieved from the cave.

His collection of old sleeping bags and some extra bedding were put down to serve as a mattress.

Each of them slept in their own sleeping bag.

Lady and Tramp seemed to know they needed to be neat.

They would go out each time Lucas had an outdoor chore. They would do their duty and come back in afterwards.

Lucas marked the calendar and went out to do his duty.

When he opened the door, he let out a shout. The snow had stopped. He could see the sun. The sky was still cloudy or hazy, but a dim sun was visible.

As the day progressed, Lucas became aware there was something very strange going on.

He asked Anna to tell him where the sun came up and where it should it set.

"It rises in the East and sets in the West," Anna said with a puzzled face.

Lucas invited everyone to come outside to watch the sunset.

They all put on their warm clothes and went out to watch the sun set.

The sun went down in a bright red glow through a veil of clouds.

"It gorgeous," Anna said as she stood next to Lucas. Clair was standing in front and between the two.

"Yes, it is, and it is setting off the East coast of the United States," Lucas said. He now knew what a key part of the Event had been.

"Are you sure," Anna asked as she looked at Lucas to see if he was joking.

"Oh, I am very sure. All my life I stood in this exact spot to watch the sunrise over the far horizon," Lucas said as he turned to lead the way back to the warmth of the cool room. The outdoor temperature was probably less than twenty degrees at the moment.

Once they were inside and were sitting together around the fire, Lucas brought up the subject again.

"I think I know what happened and where everything went. I just need to work on the idea a little more thoroughly," Lucas said as the magnitude of the event crystallized in his mind.

"Where did Mommy and Daddy end up," Clair asked as she listened to the conversation.

Lucas had not thought about Evelyn and Jim. He stopped short when Clair asked. He had been so caught up with the incredible implications of what he had just learned he had forgotten Clair's loss.

He didn't say anything. He just gave Clair a hug.

There was an old globe back in Jim and Evelyn's shelter. He would have to work this out in detail. It might prove useful in locating more material like the train wreck Anna had been in.

"Let's sing some happy songs," Lucas said as he picked his guitar.

Lucas got up early the next morning. He bundled up and went out to watch the Sunrise. The sky remained overcast with a brown or grey haze. The sun was barely visible and felt weak. It was clear whatever was in the sky was blocking the warming rays of the sun. At this rate they would miss spring and summer.

Lucas decided it was time to hike back up the trail to the train to get more of the fuel. It would be the first time he would see the wreck all at one time.

He packed a backpack with a good supply of food and took his sleeping bag. He also was pulling a sled with a fifty gallon can strapped to it. The runners of the sled were made from a pair of his snow skis. He had screwed in two pieces of wood across them and had used some more of the scrap wood in the cave to make a carrying frame for the oil barrel.

He hoped the twelve feet of show would be solid and would carry the sled. He would be using snowshoes to stay on top. He tested the snow and found it had a solid nature and would carry him on his snowshoes. The skis seemed to be holding the tank with little trouble.

Lucas was not sure he would be able to bring a full fifty gallons back, but he would try.

He hugged both Clair and Anna and told them to practice their singing while he was gone.

The trip to Jim and Evelyn's place took only an hour. The snow here was at least twelve feet deep. Lucas did not make the effort to dig down to the shelter.

He proceeded up the trail and carefully stayed to the center. He was afraid of being off the trail and accidently creating an avalanche.

He approached the train wreck and almost didn't recognize it. It was buried out of sight. He knew exactly where the diesel tank was located but it was going to be a challenge getting the fuel up to his barrel. He had used a rotating hand pump to get the previous oil out. The pump was where he had left it. He hoped it would pump oil up the ten feet that it took to reach the tank.

He rummaged around the engine compartment and found some hose that he could use.

It took him about two hours to pump the fifty gallons up to the drum on the sled.

He immediately began the journey back. As long as he kept moving the sled stayed on the surface and moved along easily. Lucas stopped for a break and almost lost the sled as it began to sink. After that Lucas kept a steady pace back to the homestead.

He now had enough fuel for several more months. He felt a sense of relief that he had been able to ensure that the three of them would continue to have the heat they so desperately needed.

He now hoped that they would be able to reestablish a way to grow the plants that would feed them.

Chapter 19: Muri, John, the Journey

Muri scratched his forty third mark on the wall of the container. The rain continued to drum on the top and sides. It was driving both he and John to the edge of insanity.

They initially were happy to get out of the rain when they crawled into the container. It turned out the container not only provided shelter, but it was also the source of food. It was a container full of canned tuna.

If they remained sane, they would be healthy survivors.

"Yes, we have all we want to eat. If all we want to eat is canned tuna," John moaned.

Other containers nearby were all locked. Neither Muri nor John could figure out a huge structure beyond the containers.

John guessed it was a container ship that had carried the container they were in.

Muri asked how a container ship would end up in the middle of Africa.

John countered with two questions. He asked where the giant rock in front of the cave had gone and where was their village and all of its people?

Muri looked at John but remained silent.

During their first few days Muri and John removed enough of the cases of tuna to create some living space.

It took only a short time for the rain to reduce their neatly stacked cases of tuna to a random pile of cans with no labels. The cardboard cases and the paper labels were reduced to the fiber they were made of and then washed away.

They re-arranged the pallets and cases inside of the container to create their living area. They had even placed one layer of cases up against the roof of the container in an attempt to muffle the noise of the pounding rain.

They utilized several pallet tie downs straps and stretched them out in the rain to an area they utilized as their latrine.

Muri had insisted that they keep the interior of the container spotless. He said that the noise of the rain was bad, but the effect of bad hygiene could be deadly.

The two systemically explored the entire area. They could not see more than a few feet in front of them, but they had used the container as the reference point and made excursions in all directions.

There was no one around.

They stopped to bless all those they had lost. They wished them well and prayed they were safe and not in the next world.

One door to the container was kept shut. One row of cases was stacked along the door from floor to ceiling. This stack went along the container wall for about three meters. A bench to sit on was formed by a single row of cases along the base.

There was enough room for both Muri and John to lay down. This became their sitting and sleeping area.

John had gathered enough dirt to fill a number of tuna cans to make a small fire ring.

They tried for almost three days to get a fire started. Muri and John's experience of getting a fire started when they went out on their adventure proved inadequate with the wood materials of the pallets.

They found one old pallet that had wood dry enough to let them get the fire going. The fresh new pallets were all too new and wet.

Muri kicked John's feet. It was quiet. The rain drumming on the container had stopped. It was eerily quiet. So quiet that he heard it!

"John, John, its stopped raining," Muri said as he nudged John awake.

Muri pushed the exit door of the container wide open and stepped out. He walked slowly around looking at a cloudy sky with the sun barely shining through, but it had stopped raining.

As Muri slowly turned around, he stopped. There was indeed a huge container ship with hundreds of containers still strapped to the deck. The container ship rested on its side.

He and John had found the container farthest from the ship. There was at least another dozen containers scattered between them and the ship.

John wondered if any of the crew might have survived.

Muri began walking toward the back of the ship where the living area and the helm was located.

Several of the containers between them and the ship were cracked or broken.

Muri stopped to check the contents of each. The rain had stripped all of the exposed material of any cardboard or paper covering. The goods of each container were distinguishable on inspection.

They had found only one other container with canned goods by the time they reached the part of the ship where the bridge and living area was located.

They had each enjoyed a can of peaches from that one container. Muri joked about their new daily menu of tuna and peaches.

The two reached the part of the ship where the ten-story high section with the bridge at the top was located. It loomed out over them and dominated the spaced above them.

Muri shouted out to see if there was anyone alive on the ship. He tried in French, English, Swahili, and Lingala. There was no response.

Muri hoisted himself over the handrail and crawled like a crab up the steep incline to some stairs going to the next level.

On several occasions their home-made rope came into good use.

Muri was the first one to reach the Bridge. The lower side door would not open, so they cross up and over to the other side door.

Two crumpled bodies lay on the lower doors.

"Well, these two never made it through the landing. I doubt we will find anyone alive but let's make a thorough search," Muri said turning to John.

They were overwhelmed as they looked out at all the containers on the deck. They stopped counting after reaching five hundred.

"Are there any working flashlights up here," John asked, "We are going to need them if we are going inside to look around.

John rummaged through the drawers of the main navigation module in the center of the room. He found the flashlights he was searching for. He also found maps, pads of paper and other items that he mentally registered.

The most interesting thing he found was a map of the ship's container layout.

Muri and John spent the rest of the day exploring the various parts of the ship. They did not find anyone alive. There were twelve bodies. They were not sure how big of a crew a ship of this size would have. It appeared something other than physical trauma killed the crew. They generally looked OK.

Muri speculated that they had suffocated. He reminded John of them passing out in the cave.

The two found the galley and a variety of food.

They also found the captain's quarters and finally located the ships armory. They found a strong steel bar and eventually broke into the armory.

"Well, we now each have excellent knives, handguns, and a rifle a piece. And we have something besides canned tuna to eat," John said as they were getting ready to leave the ship.

It was then Muri spotted the motor bikes.

He crawled up to a black Honda 300cc motorcycle. It was immaculate with not a scratch on it.

John suggested that they call it a day. They could unload the bikes the next day and use them to get a quick look around the countryside to see if there were other survivors.

The next day after a breakfast of tuna and peaches, they returned to the ship and the motorcycles.

After gathering some rope line, they selected the bikes of their choice and carefully lowered them to the ground.

They found the gas they needed in a locker located next to the bikes.

Muri spotted several wagons designed to be pulled behind the motor bikes. At first, he was going to ignore them.

When it dawned on him that the wagons were going to be essential if they found people needing help, he pointed them out to John.

John agreed but suggested that was work for the next day. It was time to try out their new toys.

The ride back up to where the river ferry crossed over to Pweto took them about an hour. The terrain was so alien that they missed the left turn where highway N5 use to be.

Muri made a pile of some debris so they could find their way back to the village location. They then turned left when they arrived at the banks of Lake Mweru and followed the shoreline.

The crossing ferry was gone, and they decided they would go into the Soweto area once they decided on a plan of action.

They back tracked and returned to the ship.

The land around them had changed significantly. Most of the loose material was sand mixed with a variety of seashells. Dirt was scarce and dispersed erratically. The old village cemetery location was now more like a beach, than a place to bury the dead.

Muri and John spent a day wrapping the bodies in canvas and lowering them off the ship onto the ground.

They dug fourteen graves side by side. There was only enough ground covering to dig the graves a little over a meter deep.

After covering the graves, John gave a brief prayer for the fourteen.

The crew was a mix of Asian, black, and white sailors. The captain looked Spanish.

They all got the same prayer and a call to God in one single ceremony.

In the same ceremony John prayed for the members of their village. Muri and he were now more certain they would never see their parents or any of the villagers again.

The morning after the burial Muri and John were on the bridge. Muri had suggested they survey the goods available to them on the ship. They needed to better understand their situation and to make some long-term plans.

John located what he called the container map. It listed the location of a container and the contents in the container. There were seven hundred and fifty containers. Eventually they would be able to get to all of the containers but in the short term most containers were inaccessible. Many were on deck and a few of those had been tossed onto the ground when the cables holding them on the deck snapped.

Muri was most interested in the containers carrying food. It turned out there were five containers of tuna. There were also containers carrying, dried milk, dried noodles, other canned fishes, bags of Indian rice and a mix of processed food products from China. The other containers carried a huge mix of goods from shoes to furniture.

John pointed out the fact that they had survived because the container they had crawled into had cans of tuna fish. If it had been a container full of shoes, they would be dead.

Muri agreed and made the point that they had all the food and materials they would ever need but they would need to get it all organized

They decided they would utilize the cloths of the sailors. The weather seemed to be cooler, and they would need warm clothes if they were to ride far on the motor bikes.

They found the rooms belonging to the owners of the motor bikes. They were able to fit into the riding clothes of the previous owners. The owners were a little larger, but the fit was adequate.

They selected the clothes they would need immediately and left the remainder where they were found.

John suggested that they utilize the containers to make themselves a village. They could arrange multiple containers with the doors all pointing inward. The open doors would overlap with the doors of the next container. Another row of containers could be placed horizontally around the top to create a second story living space.

The final touch would be a canvas roof to cover the courtyard that was created at the center.

Muri gave a laugh and asked where John was going to get the army of workers.

John pointed to the booms and a large mobile forklift secured on the deck of the ship.

Muri and John made their way to where a very large lifting unit was secured to a frame. It was not a forklift, but a hook lift intended to pick containers up by hooking to cables attached at the corner of the container and coming back to a center ring.

Muri suggested they let the equipment unload itself. He pointed to a boom that could serve as the place to hook the cable and then let the lift pick itself up, swing out and lower itself to the ground.

It was getting dark by the time the lift made it undamaged to the ground.

Muri and John decided that a celebration was in order so they opened a can of ham they found in the galley of the ship.

The village center with the single bedrock spiral served as the center of their new structure.

John suggested that first container lay in East and West direction with the opening facing the sunrise.

Muri chuckled and asked if John had noticed anything in particular about sunrise?

John looked steadily back and replied that yes, the sun was coming up from the wrong direction, but he had not wanted to worry Muri about it.

They found all the equipment they needed, and they figured out how to get it off the ship.

It did not all work smoothly. They dropped and smashed several containers as they mastered the booms and winches.

Driving the huge container lift also proved to be challenging. Several containers would forever be examples of their learning curve.

The mistakes were moved to the side for future recycling.

Muri and John looked at the seven containers that created the main circle. They had turned two containers to face each other, and their open doors served as front gates. A third container over the top of the gate containers, ensured no one would climb over the gates.

The second level of containers had over lapping doors and formed a sealed second floor crown.

Now they would be faced with emptying the containers so that they could be used to live in. They had selected the containers that had food stuff in them in hopes that it would save them some work later.

John wondered why they were building such a secure compound.

Muri reminded John on why the family had moved to their current location and now they were alone.

John nodded his agreement.

Muri was especially proud of the center piece of the compound. He and John had removed it piece by piece from the ship's galley. It had taken them two days to disconnect, dismantle and move the eight-burner stove with a flat steel plate in the middle with ovens at each end, to its current location.

The large gas tank, though much more dangerous to handle was easily reached with their container sky hook and moved to its place between two of the containers.

Muri asked John to be the first to light the stove. He was going to prepare their first cooked meal. It would be noodles, with shrimp mixed with cooked seaweed.

The next day Muri cursed as he fought to secure the canvas roof covering to the cable support structure he and John had set up. It was taking longer, and it was more work than he had imagined.

Thick cables running from the corners of each container on the second level connected to a support pole in the center of the compound had gone up quickly as had the top and bottom cables forming the edges for connecting the canvas.

John and he had secured hooks on the top and bottoms of the canvas an in sections lift them up and hooked them onto the cables.

Everything went as they had planned but it was their small size and lack of strength that made handling the bulky canvas to difficult.

They each got very good at using their giant container lift with a feathers touch.

Once they had the "roof" over the compound they stacked most of the contents from one of the containers into the compound.

They arranged the interior, so they had two sleeping areas and a common sitting area. Their bedrooms, and the sitting area was furnished with the furniture from the ship.

The ship's deck chairs were placed out in the main circle.

John found and positioned several large tanks on the second level and guided the rainwater into them with some troughs.

After a few rains they realized the water needed filtering. Muri located the ship's on-board charcoal filtering system and moved it to the compound.

Both John and Muri had discussed trying to get the ships radio working.

They mounted the antenna to the top of the post at the center of the compound and placed the radio center in the container next to theirs.

The gas-powered generator located between the two containers was running smoothly. The radio transmitter came on and Muri made the first announcement.

This is Mweru Station, Mweru Station standing by. Anyone hearing this please reply.

He repeated this on multiple frequencies.

He went through all the channels to see if anyone else was broadcasting.

Muri and John discussed going out in search of other survivors.

They agreed that they needed to get themselves organized for the long term and to decide how and where to search for survivors.

They realized that when they went out to find people, they might find very desperate people needing food.

John and Muri finally off loaded the wagons designed to be pulled behind the motorcycles.

Each bike could pull two of the wagons.

They remembered and retrieved the bikers clothing they had left on the ship.

The two discussed and prepared for every eventuality they could imagine.

Finally, they were ready to venture out and seek to find and help any survivors they could.

They did not know it at the time, but they would later be recognized as the builders of a new country.

Chapter 20: Cualli, Tosi, the Lucky Lady

Tosi counted the scratch marks where she kept track of the days. This was a morning ritual she had started on the very first day.

The rain was unrelenting, but it slowly became cleaner.

She had turned the hide of the calf into two sleeveless jackets and a pair of leather shorts for each of them. She had used the scrapings of the old coconut mixed in water to treat the hides and had been surprised at her success at keeping the leather flexible.

She looked at Cualli and complemented him for his great looking outfit.

Cualli laughed and replied that it had been made by a virgin goddess.

Cualli and Tosi discussed the Event and what had happened and how they had survived and no one else had.

Cualli speculated that when he had pushed off the alter, he had launched the two of them to into a higher altitude. This meant they would have fallen from a greater height but in their descent, they had crossed more of the ocean below them.

He and Tosi had landed close enough to an island where the others, if any survived had landed sooner but farther from the island.

Tosi looked up from some old coconuts that were sprouting and sending out some roots. There was no shortage of moisture for their exposed roots.

Tosi commented that the others also did not have someone who wanted to stay alive as much as the person who saved her.

Cualli looked back at her and bowed his head.

He looked at Tosi and smiled. He was happy that Tosi enjoyed raising the coconuts.

He was sure they would never yield any coconuts in time to help them survive but they would be seeding the future with them.

She was also friends with about a dozen red crabs that shared the shelter with them. The smallest was about hand size and the largest about the size of a dinner plate. Their claws were fierce looking and worried Cualli.

The crabs seemed to be fighting the rain almost as much as they were. Each crab would go out for some time but would always return and take refuge in the dry overhang. They seem to respect the space separation and stayed together away from the two of them.

Tosi woke up. It was still dark, but it was quiet.

She immediately woke Cualli.

They looked at each other and took in the silence.

He could hear the waves. The rain had stopped. It was still dark, but the rain had stopped.

He and Tosi walked along the edge of the overhang. A few drops of water were still dripping from the edge.

They walked out and down to the beach. Arm in arm they walked around the island. They watched as the day came over the horizon.

Tosi pointed out some islands that were out in the distant horizon. The sky still had a grey covering. The sun was a faint light barely shining through.

Tosi pointed out the dolphins in the lagoon. She asked Cualli whether he thought they had enough food in the Lagoon. She suggested they look for a way for them to get out of the lagoon.

If their cave was high noon, they found a low spot at the nine position that with a little work they would be able to open a channel to let the dolphins out.

Cualli found a wooden plank. He tied a rope to it like you tie a rope to a tree swing. This allowed them to each pull on the board. Together they pulled the plank and moved the sand to one side like a bulldozer

They started their effort on the lagoon side and worked their way toward the ocean. They learned quickly to angle the board at about a thirty-degree angle as they pulled the sand into the lagoon. The work went amazingly fast.

They learned to control the angle in both the left and right plane but also the forward and backward plane. The two laughed as they played bulldozer and opened up a six-foot-wide channel out of the lagoon. They were only able to get the channel to be two feet deep.

The two dolphins had been watching, chirping, and clicking as if cheering them on. When the channel finally broke out to the ocean, they were right there and shuffled past Tosi and Cualli and made their way into the ocean.

It was clear to that the dolphins were extremely hungry.

Tosi and Cualli returned to their shelter for a quick lunch.

Then they decided to walk around the island again.

This time they noticed the large amount of debris that was washing up on the shore. There seemed to be a random offering from home products stores, clothing stores and hardware stores.

Then they were shocked when they found several decomposing bodies.

Cualli, held Tosi to him and said in a matter-of-fact voice that all the people at their last show probably died somewhere out in the ocean and that they were lucky.

Tosi wanted to know what they were going to do as she turned and looked at their steps leading back to their shelter.

Cualli pointed to the opposite side of the island to indicate where they would bury the bodies. He just hoped there would not be too many.

He began to look for something to dig with and a way to move the bodies to the burial location.

Tosi spotted the white hull of a catamaran. She estimated it to be about twenty feet long. It was couple of hundred yards off the beach laying on its side.

Cualli suggested they swim out to it and see if it was in good enough shape to salvage.

The blue main sail was fully deployed but everything seemed to be in good shape. They worked together to get the sail down and rolled up on the boom. Cualli pulled the center board up.

He tied ropes to the rail on the underwater side. They each took one side of the mast rope.

Cualli maneuvered the cat, so the mast was pointed at the oncoming waves. They both leaned as far back as possible and managed to lift the mast top clear as the next wave approached. The wave and their weight were just enough for the cat to right itself.

The wave carried the boat toward the shore. Cualli pushed Tosi onboard the cat and told her to steer it up on the shore.

He half swam and was half pulled until his feet finally found the bottom. He then pulled the cat on the beach and collapsed.

Cualli lay with the rope tied around his waist. Tosi sat down beside him. Together the two looked at their grand prize.

Tosi made the point that now they could go to the other Islands they had spotted.

Cualli suggested they spend the rest the day making sure they had a secure place to keep the catamaran.

Tosi suggested they put the cat in the inner lagoon. They would need to dig their channel a little bit wider and somewhat deeper.

They pulled the cat to the opening and anchored it so they could judge how much digging they would need to do.

Ok, let's cancel all our other appointments for the day and get this baby into the lagoon.

Cualli mentioned that they needed to name the boat. Tosi pointed to the name painted on each side on the outside of each hull.

She made the point that the boat had an appropriate name. *"Lucky Lady."*

She was about twenty-five feet long and fifteen feet wide. It took Cualli and Tosi two days to dig the entrance out wide and deep enough to get her into the inner lagoon.

It was not an ocean-going size, but it would do to get to the islands they saw on the horizon.

Tosi looked out at the Lucky Lady as she inventoried the articles, they had carried up each morning from the beach. Cualli was out searching the beach for newly washed in objects and materials.

Cualli piled the tremendous amount of waste into large piles.

He and Tosi buried seventeen people of every age and gender. This was always a gruesome experience. Cualli did most of the work in putting the bodies on heavy plastic sheets and dragging them to the burial site. He had found a shovel that made digging the graves easy.

He always waited to the end and then summed Tosi to say a prayer to for the dead.

"I don't know how we made it. I wonder how many people died. What do you think happened to our families," Tosi asked as they ate their dinner?

"I don't know. I hope they are alright and if they are, I hope they don't worry about us. There is no way to know. All I know is we have each other, and we are going to make it," Cualli replied as he gave Tosi a hug.

The food stuff was mostly what they would have considered junk food, but it was contained in plastic. Tosi found a case of dried noodles. Cualli found a rack that had different kinds of beef jerky. A liter bottle of orange soda was another prize.

Tosi declared that it was time to go and explore the other islands.

Cualli strategically planted the palm trees so they would bracket the path on each side. It they ever came back there might be palm shade and coconuts.

Both of them said goodbye to their crab friends. There was now a slew of little red crabs. They were making a comeback.

Cualli looked at all the piles of trash he had accumulated around the island. He was concerned about some future storm blowing it all back out to sea.

He informed Tosi that he was going to burn it before they left.

Together they pulled the Lucky Lady out of the lagoon and anchored her just off the beach.

They carried out their meager belongings and the food and drinks they had salvaged.

There were tears in Tosi's eyes as the climbed-on board after the last load was on.

Cualli pulled in the anchor, lowered the center board part way, and pulled the main sail halfway up the mast.

He turned the *Lucky Lady*, so the sail caught the wind.

He looked back and whispered a prayer of thanks.

Chapter 21: New Home

The spring did not bring the warmth needed to melt off the snow. Lucas would not be able to plant the garden.

Besides keeping the area outside the cool room clear of snow, Lucas had dug a path back to the cave and another up to the corner of the garden to where the spring still gurgle up out of the ground. The spring was the source of fresh water for drinking and cooking. The snow still had a brackish taste to it.

There was no indication of life in Buchanan. In the past he had been able to see the lights of the town from the top of his driveway. There were no lights. There was no smoke. There was no sign of life.

When Lucas announced he wanted to go down to Buchanan, Anna jumped at the chance of getting to see more than the cool room, the cave, and the flat area in between the two.

Her leg had healed well, and she was ready for some way to release her cabin fever.

Lucas agreed that it would be good for all of them to go together.

Lucas new immediately that it had been the right decision both Clair and Anna went around singing and joking. The energy between all of them had gone up tenfold.

That evening the guitar playing and singing had new energy. Lucas was aware how much better he was playing and the improvement that Anna had made in his ability to carry a tune.

He went about making some snowshoes for Anna and Clair.

He prepared a backpack for each of them. His pack contained a two-person tent, the large sleeping bag and most of the heavy food. He figured the three would crowd into the one bag and tent and be able to stay warm.

Both Clair and Anna carried back packs filled with food. He gave each of them a walking stick.

He presented Anna with a walking stick with her initials engraved at the top end of the stick and a B1 below it. He let Anna know that her stick would serve as the front pole of their tent and that B1 indicated the first hiking trip to Buchanan.

He presented Clair with a smaller walking stick and let her know that her stick would hold up the other end of their tent.

When Clair asked about his walking stick and what it would be used for, Lucas laughed and said he would use his walking stick to fight off the bears. He did show the freshly carve B1AC that was far down on the walking stick.

He explained that it meant first trip to Buchanan with Anna and Clair. He was surprised when he realized he was getting tears in his eyes. He seemed to be reliving the recent experiences that they had all shared.

Anna could see that the simple ceremony of presenting the walking sticks had emotionally touched Lucas. She waited a few moments while he rummaged around in his backpack as he regained his composure.

Then she thanked Lucas for her walking stick and gave him a light kiss. Anna was surprised by the current that passed through her as she gave Lucas what had been intended as a light thank you kiss.

She had never experienced the feeling she had at that instant. It was the first time she realized what their time together had meant to her. Fate had dropped her into the hands of Mr. Right. She hoped Lucas shared similar emotions.

Me too, Clair said and got a kiss from Anna as the three hugged each other.

The next day was a calm but still a cloudy day. It was a cold thirty-five degrees.

The day before their hike Lucas gave both Anna and Clair some lessons on walking in snowshoes. Clair was light enough that she barely needed to be in snowshoes. Both Anna and Clair moved easily over the snow. The snowshoes were most beneficial to the one who was carrying a heavy backpack.

He stressed that there was no hurry and the coming back would take three times as long as going down.

Lucas had waited until the last moment to announce that Lady and Tramp would be left at the homestead site.

He had come to this decision when he had seen them get stuck in the snow. There was no way to take them. He was surprised when Clair did not object but instead talk to the two dogs and explained how hard it was for them to get through the snow.

Early the next morning after a hearty breakfast the three started out just as the sun rose in the west. The hike down the lane warned Lucas immediately. It was clear the hike would be tougher than he had anticipated. By the time they reached the bottom of the lane to the point where Grey Ridge Road began, it was obvious they would not make it down in one day.

It was about six miles on the highway to Buchanan, but it was going to be rough going. The highway itself seemed to be missing and the snow was still several feet deep.

About a mile toward Buchanan, they were blocked by a pile of debris that erased any idea about making it to Buchanan at all.

Lucas had no idea what lay before them. It looked like a mixture of lumber yard materials mixed with auto parts and the remnants of a clothing store.

Anna picked up a piece of paper sticking out of the snow. It was written in Brazilian Portuguese.

"I think this comes from Brazil," Anna declared.

Lucas found a place on the uphill sided of the road. He took off his backpack. He asked Anna and Clair to do the same.

He had decided that this would be their first camp location.

Lucas looked at the mountain of material that lay in front of them. He was conscious of the fact that along with the materials there were probably dead and decomposing bodies.

He asked Anna and Clair to stay at their camp position until he checked out the situation.

Lucas entered into the maze before him. He unconsciously began to organize the items he found. There seemed to be a large amount of canned goods.

Then he came to an all-terrain vehicle on its side. He pushed it up right and checked out its condition. It was filled with gas and the oil was at level. He was surprised at the growl of the engine when he turned the key. He let it run for a few moments then shut the engine off.

He would need to clear a way through the debris to get the vehicle out. On his return Lucas spotted several bodies that were trapped in the rubble. He was sure there would be more since he now believed he was in the middle of a shopping mall.

He brought several of the leaflets and paper he had found back to the Anna. She looked at them and declared that this was a shopping center in Guaratingueta, a city between Rio and Sao Paulo.

Lucas asked Anna and Clair to stay in camp and sort the materials he would bring to them. Ann was about to object, but Lucas finished his explanation with the fact that there were Angels in the rubble, and he would take care of them himself.

Anna immediately understood the situation and agreed to stay with Clair and clean and sort the materials Lucas would bring to them.

She also suggested they take time to have a sandwich and get organized before Lucas continued.

Lucas was actually hungry and quickly agreed to a snack. He shared the news about having found a functional all-terrain vehicle. He would bring it out first so they could use it to take the items they decided to keep back to the home stead.

When Lucas re-entered the jumble, he made a point of opening up a path through which he would bring the vehicle out.

On his return he found a black, heavy gauge flat-bed wagon designed to be pulled by the all-terrain vehicle. It appeared to Lucas that the two items had been on display and for sale.

He searched around for a gas can and was overjoyed to find a red plastic container filled with gas.

Lucas continued on beyond the vehicle and wagon and made a more thorough examination of the jumble of material.

He counted fifty-three bodies in various stages of decomposition.

He spotted what he thought was a gasoline truck but could not get back to examine it.

He decided that he would return later on his own and take the time to bury the bodies. Then he would continue to sort through the rubble.

For now, he would load the all-terrain with food and other materials and get it all back up to the homestead.

Lucas was about to start up the vehicle when he heard a meow. He followed his ears to where a mother calico cat was nursing three kittens. The mother cat's frail condition made it obvious she had not eaten much of anything.

Lucas put the mother cat and three kittens into a square plastic storage container and put the box in the seat next to him.

He took the time to load the back of the vehicle and the wagon with the food stuff that he had found and set aside.

On his return to Anna and Clair, Lucas announced that the mountain of rubble was a gold mine for them. He let them know that it would provide all the materials they would need to build a new home at the homestead.

Anna asked about Angels and Lucas replied that there were so many that he would need to come back at another time to see how to handle the situation.

Lucas threw the back packs onto the wagon and the three began their journey back to the homestead and the cool room.

The steep incline up toward the homestead, the snow and the load were too much for the all-terrain vehicle. Lucas got out and let Anna drive. Once he got out the all-terrain vehicle was able to pull the load up the long driveway to the homestead flat.

Lucas trudged back to the homestead flat on his snowshoes.

He arrived to find most of the goods unloaded and sorted out in front of the cool room door.

Clair had taken the cat and kittens into the cool room where she was introducing them to Lady and Tramp.

Lucas chuckled when he heard the cat hissing and Clair telling her to relax, and that Lady and Tramp were kind.

Lucas shared that he would be able to build a new home and replace the barn and work shed with all the material he had seen in the wreckage below.

Anna looked up from sorting the food cans. She could see that Lucas had found new energy and they all seemed to have a new sense of hope.

Lucas looked around the homestead flat. He was going to build himself the work shed he had always wanted. He also planned to build a greenhouse to go with it.

He announced his intensions and asked if Anna and Clair would help him rebuild the homestead.

In the following days, Lucas cleared the way from the homestead to the jumble on the road.

On each trip he would bring back the lumber and building materials he needed to build a work shed.

He continued to search through the jumble.

He carefully moved the bodies to a place by the road that would serve as a graveyard. He would wrap the remains in some black plastic sheeting where he found them and leave them to be moved at the end of each day.

Lucas stood looking at the gasoline tanker. Its tires had burst. The truck it had been pulled by was nowhere to be found.

He found the gauges in the back and after looking at the gauges he determined it was full of gasoline.

He was overjoyed. This amount of fuel meant he would be able to power his electrical generators and fuel his new vehicle for years to come.

He found two new queen size beds with their mattresses still sealed in a thick plastic covering.

He immediately stopped his work for the day and took them up to the homestead flat. He cleared the makeshift sleeping area and set up the two beds.

Lucas watched as Anna and Clair made the beds with some new sheets they had found. The sleeping bags served as the blankets.

Lucas declared it was bedtime as soon they had cleaned up after dinner.

Anna laughed and insisted they take a moment to sing together before going to sleep.

Lucas made it a point to move as much of the building materials he could up to the homestead. He found the entire spectrum of major timber and all cuts of wood down to finishing trim.

He concluded that one of the businesses must have been a wood yard or hardware center.

He quickly designed and constructed what he called his workshop. It was a thirty-by-thirty square structure.

He built a three foot by six-foot worktable that he used as a desk.

Each day was split in two. The morning was spent working the jumble on the highway. The afternoon was spent building the homestead.

Anna split her time as well. Some days she would accompany Lucas to the jumble.

Every day she and Clair held school class in the morning, and later they would sort and inventory the goods that had been found.

Together he and Anna were designing the new house that would-be built-in front of the cool room. Lucas was standing at the desk reviewing the drawing.

Anna entered holding a cup of Jasmine tea.

Lucas stopped in shock. For a moment as Anna walked through the door the bright light behind her blurred her features. The sight of Amanda flashed before him. He hoped it had ended painlessly for Amanda.

Anna asked if he was alright.

You look lovely this afternoon. Thanks for the tea.

He did not know when it had happened, but he knew Anna and he had become soul mates. They would get through together.

It was clear to Lucas that the weather was not going to allow him to plant his garden any time soon. He spent the next month designing and building his greenhouse.

The green house was one hundred feet long and twenty feet wide. There were major support posts standing six feet above the ground every four feet. Curved one-inch stainless steel piping supported a clear overlapping plastic roof.

Lucas only built a few of the twenty gardening tables planned for the green house. He needed some immediately so he could germinate some of the plants.

This would allow him to grow a few items and to keep his seed supply fresh.

The next day Lucas took the ATV and made his way to the river. There was nothing but the bridge support in the middle of the river. The Mayor had always been proud of the fact that the support was anchored in the bedrock.

Lucas later returned with Anna and Clair to place a placard to commemorate his friends and the people of Buchanan. He thought of Jeff and Rachel and wished them peace.

<u>Chapter 22: The Garden</u>

*L*ucas walked slowly beneath the clear plastic cover that effectively passed the feebly sunlight heat through the curved roof and efficiently held it in. The forty-yard-long and ten-yard-wide green house filled to the brim with plants of every sort was earning its name. It had become the main source of fresh produce.

Twenty, two-foot-wide troughs with a miserly mix of sand, glass pellets, pebbles and marbles ran along the interior guiding the nutrient water passed the roots of the plant extended across the width of the green house. The troughs received a nutrient stream from a nutrient, water supply faucet on one end. Each trough had a slight tilt to ensure a slow steady flow of the rich water past the plant root system.

Lucas knew that he was using a combination of wicking and nutrient bath hydroponic gardening. It was a combination system based on the situation versus a design of choice. It worked so he was satisfied.

A fifty-gallon nutrient supply barrel mounted near the top of arc of the green house roof provided the fluid distribution head. The nutrient return barrel was at floor level and the nutrient make up barrel was mounted just above the return barrel. Lucas used a third barrel to supply the make-up nutrient fluid.

Located at the center of the greenhouse, the entire system was designed to be gravity powered. Power was only needed at the nutrient water supply and return point.

A mechanical windmill powered pumping system with a human powered backup was the primary way the system functioned. A small electric sump pump powered by a gas-powered electric generator was the back up.

The green house had come online during the first missing summer. It had produced a crop every three months for the last year. It was now entering its second year fully functional with close to one hundred percent utilization.

All three of them spent a good deal of time keeping everything in order and producing. They were all surprised and pleased that the plants did so well, grew much faster than expected and the yield was much more abundant than they had dreamt about.

Lucas had no idea of the exact water, fertilizer mix. He had a limited supply of fertilizer that he had recovered from the pile of debris down on the road, so he used as little as possible. The plants flourished so he kept it at the lowest level he possible could.

The brackish water reclaimed from melting the snow seem to provide some nutrients as well.

Lucas's use of hydroponics in the green house was one of survival. There was plenty of canned and processed food for short term but a fresh tomato, a succulent bell pepper, a crunchy carrot or a fresh pickle was not something they could go to grocery store to buy. In the long-term Lucas knew he needed this green house and the garden still laying under a foot of snow.

The garden remained unplanted and remained under the snow for the second season. He had managed to arrange the new soil that had dropped down onto the mountain. This soil was reddish and of a different nature.

Lucas was not sure how good of a garden he would have if he ever got to plant it.

Anna let him know that it was the dirt from Brasil, and she thought it would be good dirt.

The first recovery priority had been food. The second priority had been the building materials to rebuild the homestead. The third priority had been fuel. Sorting through the rubble had been like mining for gold.

Lucas had also recovered a substantial amount of canned goods, food goods sealed in plastic warps, and dried foods, spices, cereals. There was almost a two-year supply of processed meat. He thought of the find as all the items in a large grocery.

The cool room and the cave held most of the food. Some overflow was stored under the green house tables.

He recovered almost all the lumber from a working Hardware – Lumber store.

He had all the windows, doors, treated lumber, beams that he would ever need. He built another shed to store all the building materials and tools.

Lucas took extra care of the gasoline truck full of fuel. He left the truck where he found it and worked around it. He built a lean to shed that protected the dispensing hose and nozzle. He painted a sign, "Mayfield Gas Station" and held a grand opening for Anna and Clair.

Lucas came out of the "work shed" that served as his office and walked across the yard toward the home that he, Anna, and Clair had designed and built.

Even though the weather was on the cold side, Anna was chasing Clair around the veranda that ran around the entire house.

Their new home was a single-story ranch built three feet above the ground with a gravity powered water supply and drainage system.

The kitchen center, facing the cool room was a design encompassing old technology with the thought and room to install new technology in the future.

The cooking oven system was designed to be fueled externally from the veranda. The veranda extended to the cool room door. The cool room was the "refrigerator" of the house.

The kitchen was fully outfitted with a gas range, a double two door refrigerator with the bottom halve freezer. The only issue with both items was that there was not enough electrical power to use the refrigerator and they did not have the gas for the stove.

The counter tops were of Brazilian granite that was black with flecks of green, and gold. The edges were rough because they did not have the tools to polish it, but Lucas had managed to match the cut edges were granite met granite on the center kitchen island and the length of the counters.

The floor was a white and black speckled marble. They were loose tile on a flat wooden base. The tile might one day get set in the proper cement.

The front half of the house was a great room with windows all the way around and half inch hardwood floor.

There were two bedrooms on each side of the house. Each pair of bedrooms shared one bathroom.

The entire house was raised three feet above the flat to allow for a gravity drain. A platform built on top of the cool room held a water tank and a small windmill powered the pump that filled the water tank.

There were hanging bench swings near the corners on the front veranda and a round table with chairs at each end of the house. The veranda in back was used for storing a variety of supplies.

Each bedroom had a set of sliding doors opening up out to the veranda.

There were no ceilings for any of the rooms. The roof supported by center beams and beams running to the side walls had light boxes over each of the rooms. The house felt very open, and they hoped eventually Sunlight filled.

Using the recovered furniture Anna and Clair furnished the house. Most of the furniture needed total reworking. These became projects that the three did together. They had the time, and they had the materials to repair and refinish many of the pieces they needed.

Lucas enjoyed these work sessions and afterwards there was a story about each piece.

Lucas captured several rabbits when he was clearing the debris. They were not the standard wild rabbit of the area. They were a chocolate color, domesticated breed and seemed tame. They needed food when he broke into their den as he cleared up some debris.

They had become somewhat wild, and it took him several days to round up three females, two males. There were an additional three younger rabbits.

The three females had produced three litters each. He selected half as breeding stock, twenty five percent became fresh meat, and he was trying to release the remainder.

He made a point of providing some food for the freed rabbits. He was not sure there was enough food for them in the surrounding countryside.

Periodically finding another decomposing body continued to shock Lucas. He would never get over finding and burying more than two hundred people.

He had created a cemetery along what had been the road. A small backhoe recovered from the same pile as the bodies made it possible for Lucas to dig and bury so many bodies. When he buried one body, he immediately dug the next greave. If he found multiple bodies, he would dig all the graves prior to moving them. It was gruesome work.

He would always check to see if there was some identification on or around the body. Eight percent of the graves had markers with names. Lucas had simply numbered the remains with numbers and dates.

Each Sunday Anna, Clair and he would walk down to the cemetery hold a short prayer service and then Lucas would play the guitar and they would sing a song.

Clair let Anna and Lucas know that she had known about the dead from the first day when the two talked about the Angels that Lucas had found.

Lucas smiled and gave Clair a hug.

"I still think of them as Angels. It makes it easier to bury them and not get too emotional," Lucas said quietly.

It was nearing the end of June when Lucas came out to sit on the veranda and suddenly realized that he was looking at a blue sky.

He immediately called to Anna and Clair to come and join him. The two came running out thinking some catastrophe was happening.

Anna asked why he had called.

Lucas simply pointed up into the sky.

Clair immediately spotted the change and kept telling everyone to look at the sun.

Tears came into Anna's eyes, and she walked over to Lucas and put her arms around his waist and leaned against him as she looked up at the sun.

"We are so fortunate," she said quietly and pulled Clair to her chest.

The next day Lucas took Anna and Clair down to what had been Grey Ridge Road to a field where he had parked over two hundred functioning cars, pickups, vans, and delivery trucks.

Lucas indicated about twenty that he had driven in and those that had been pulled in with the small tow truck. He had disconnected the batteries of all the vehicles.

Anna looked at all the cars and wondered what they were going to do with all of them.

Lucas commented that he had brought them down to help him select the vehicle that they would use for their exploration trip. He took them to the three he had lined up as the most probable ones.

The next day at lunch Lucas carried in a radio transmitter and receiver. He had found it in a crumpled building and had almost passed it by but then he thought about how it might be used to connect with other survivors.

He had carefully extracted all the wiring, the microphones, the volume control boards, the transmitter, receiver, speaker, and the antennas.

Lucas and Anna agreed that raising the roof over his work area and putting in a second floor would be the quickest way to create a space for their radio station.

Lucas and Anna both noticed how the project to create their radio station had captured Clair's interest and enthusiasm.

Lucas suggested to Clair that she should become the station master.

Clair wanted to know what a station master did.

Anna replied that a station master was responsible for the programs and the content that was broadcast, and that person would also be responsible to talk with any contacts that might be made.

Lucas and Anna smiled at each other when Clair smiled and agreed to become the station master of "Homestead Garden Station."

Anna complimented Clair on giving the station such a great name. "And what is the content that will be transmitted," Lucas asked?

Clair's earnest reply was first I will announce the station name. Then I will give them the news of the day. This will be followed by a message of inspiration, and we will close with us singing to them.

Do I still have to do my homework and chores? Clair asked with a smile.

It was almost a month later that Homestead Garden Station went on the air.

After breakfast they all went to the station broadcast room.

"This is Clair Egelston, Master of the Homestead Garden Station. This is our inaugural transmission. If you hear this broadcast please contact us after our program," Clair spoke slowly and clearly.

The daily format for this program will consist of the News, the good news or inspiration and a song from the famous Homestead Trio Singers. Feel free to suggest programing improvements but hold any negative comments about the singing.

By now most of my listeners will know that North is now South, and East is now West. You are also aware at how fortunate you are to be listening at all. Welcome to the new world.

Clair winked at Anna and Lucas.

Anna and Lucas were looking at each other with broad smiles. Clair was blowing them away.

The good news is the Sun is shining. It seems that two years of winter is coming to an end. Our garden is planted, our greenhouse is full, the rabbits are proliferating, and my dogs get along with the cat and the kittens. Clair continued in a slow and steady voice. It was clear she had practiced.

The song we are going to sing is "This Land."

Lucas led off with a guitar intro and the three of them sang their song.

Lucas was praising Clair on being so professional on the air when a faint, but clear voice came over the radio.

"Home Garden Station this is Earl in new Southwest, East Coast, Puget Sound. Come in please.

The three stopped in surprise. They had not really expected such a quick response.

They all stood for a moment staring at the radio.

Clair recovered first and replied, "This is Clair responding to Earl at Puget Sound Station. I am very pleased to make contact with you."

Earl responded that Clair sounded like an Angel to him.

Clair, Lucas, and Anna all laughed simultaneously at Clair being called an Angel.

Clair replied, "Our Angels are in heaven, and I am still alive and well, in the Mountains of Virginia. Here we bury our Angels."

Earl replied quietly that he knew what she meant and that there have been so many Angels out where he was. There are only six of us here at Puget Sound where there were millions. You are our first contact. We were getting a little lonely and paranoid. Thanks for the news and for that great song. I would like to do a few rounds with your guitarist.

How many survivors are there in your location?

Thank you for the complement. Together we make nine.

Suddenly a much stronger voice broke in.

"Puget Sound, Garden Station, this is Harrisburg, welcome to the air. This is Nathan, we are twenty and needy. We could use some food. Can Garden Station help?"

Clair looked at Lucas,

"Do you want to respond? Can we help," Clair asked?

"You're the station master and you are doing a great job. You respond. Find out what they need and when do they need it. Don't let them know of our exact location," Lucas coached Clair.

"This is Garden Station, please state your needs and timing, we will see if we can help," Clair responded.

In the following week contact was made with six more stations. The ones on the edges of the transmission range each had additional contacts. Together Clair and Anna plotted the web of stations. It reached almost all the way around the world. One station was in the middle of the Pacific.

The connections only represented two hundred twenty people. This was a shock.

Only a few hundred people. The scale of the Event was mind numbing.

Chapter 23: Contact

Lucas walked down the rows of vehicles to where he had parked the utility and work vehicles. He was looking for the ice cream truck.

He walked by a heavy-duty trailer and made a mental note to inspect it and see if it was in good condition. He wanted to tow it behind the black GMC SUV he had selected.

Lucas wanted the speakers and the transmitter from the ice cream truck.

Lucas had a large supply of wheels, tires, rims, and other car parts stored in several of the trailers parked in this same location.

A week later Lucas surveyed the truck, trailer, spare wheels for both the large black SUV and the trailer. There was a row of gas cans along the top of the trailer. The extra wheels were mounted on top of the SUV. The broadcast speaker from the ice cream truck was mounted on a bar that held the wheels on the roof.

He had spent the week preparing the SUV and the trailer. Anna and Clair had calculated how much thirty people needed and were surprised at the amount.

"These people need to plant a garden. We can help them once, but they will quickly wipe out our supply," Anna brought up during their dinner the evening before their departure.

"I agree we will need to make this clear to them. I wonder how they have managed to sustain themselves so far," Lucas replied.

The next morning, Lucas walked around giving the SUV and trailer a final inspection. The trailer was full of the basic necessities Anna had decided would be shared. There were twenty bags of rice, and twenty bags of black beans. She had included twenty cured hams. Twenty pounds of salt and a matching volume of black pepper. She had included a large bag of small hot peppers. A variety of canned goods by the case made up the rest of the order.

Lucas joked about Anna getting stuck on twenty.

She was more serious in her reply about her alarm at dealing with thirty people they did not know.

She wanted to take a rifle along for protection.

Lucas was surprised. He voiced his concern about them not having time to practice with a rifle.

Anna insisted and shared that she was an expert marksman. She wanted a rifle with the scope that was stored in the gun closet.

She spent the evening before leaving, demonstrating her skill by shooting stones off of the tops of wooden stakes Lucas had set up.

"When we get back you will have to teach us how to shoot as well as you do," Lucas complimented Anna.

Why do we need to be able to shoot," Clair asked?

"We may meet unfriendly people. They may threaten or try to harm us. We need to be prepared for such a situation.

We should also take the time to practice Tae Kwon Do and Aikido. We should think about doing that after we get back from this trip," Lucas explained.

"I have a red belt in Tae Kwon Do," Anna declared.

"Wow then we are two thirds of the way there. I got my first-degree black belt before I moved back to the homestead. We just need to practice," Lucas said.

He was surprised that after two years together they were just finding out these facts about each other.

"I don't know what you are talking about," Clair said feeling a little left out.

She exclaimed that the only belt she had was the one holding up her blue jeans.

The three had discussed how to arrange the interior of the SUV.

Clair had the back seat behind the driver's side. Lady would sit with her. The radio equipment and speaker controls were behind the passenger's side. It was positioned so Clair could easily use it.

The back was mostly left open for sleeping. Lucas had built a frame so two people could sleep one above the other. This left one side for clothes and a small refrigerator.

Anna had the right front seat and Tramp had the position between them.

They were almost ready to depart.

Lucas loaded a dozen boxes of what they considered care packages they hoped to give to any random survivors they might meet.

"We are equipped for our "Vacation," Lucas commented as he got into the driver's seat.

The entire trip would be attempted using whatever was left of Interstate Highway 81. Clair had studied the maps they had and had calculated the miles

"By my calculations we have about two hundred seventy-five miles. We should pass through about ten towns and cities. There should be a population of some three hundred thousand between us and where we are going.

They went slowly past the graveyard as they made their way past the ruble on the way to Buchanan.

The white vertical markers pointing upward in silence to a blue sky were reminders of the fate these people had suffered.

I hope we find more than Angels," Clair said from the back seat as she took in the graveyard.

"When do you think you will have gone through all the rubble," Anna asked as she looked at the immense size of what remained.

"I have no clue," Lucas replied.

"Even after all we have utilized it looks like we haven't made a dent in it," Anna continued.

There was still food and other valuable materials to extract but there was other work at the homestead as well. Also, every time he came down, he had to bury several people. Finding them and burying them always took a toll.

Anna knew how hard it was for Lucas to come down and constantly need to stop and bury the Angels he found.

Lucas made the drive down the mountain to Eighty-One and as expected nothing was left. It was now a barren very different terrain. His speed on what was left of the highway was seldom above ten miles per hour.

He commented over his shoulder to Clair that her estimate of traveling at fifteen miles per hour might be too high.

Clair started her call for survivors as they approached the location of the first small town that bordered the highway.

She was in her element when she had the microphone in her hand.

Lucas pointed out that if they did find anyone, or a group, he would stop the SUV and go to talk with the survivors. Anna would stand by with the rifle.

Anna asked why Lucas was so worried.

He pointed out that they might meet some very desperate people that might attack them to get to the food.

Anna understood and was glad that she had convinced Lucas about her bringing the rifle.

She believed he would have brought the rifle for himself because she had seen him cleaning it and getting it ready. She knew he had not wanted to alarm her or ask her to do something she did not want too. She realized that they had so much to learn about each other.

Anna reached over and put her hand on Lucas's cheek.

He looked at her and smiled.

Suddenly Clair shouted for them to slow down. Someone was waving a flag, or some object and was running toward them in the field off to their right side.

Lucas looked quickly around as he stopped the SUV.

I am going to go and meet with this person.

"You out in the field stop running toward us. Lower and raise your

flag twice to show you understand," Clair said in a commanding tone of voice.

The figure stopped and did as he was told.

"How many are there with you. Raise and lower your flag once for each person," Clair continued.

Lucas reached back patted Clair on the back and told her what a good job she was doing.

Lucas scanned the surroundings as he went to the trailer and picked up a box prepared to last a six-person group for a week.

He walked slowly toward the single person in the field.

He looked over at Anna who stood outside of the SUV with her rifle in hand. Both of them had decided to wear bullet proof vests for this occasion.

Lucas took in the skinny, emaciated person that was probably fifteen years old.

He ask slowly and distinctly where the rest of the people were.

"They are back in camp," was the reply. "We have each been trying to find food. We ran out a few days ago and decided we needed to move on."

Lucas asked his name. It was Larry.

"Larry, I am Lucas. For now, please stay where you are. I am going to leave a box of food that will last all of you for a week.

I will leave and you must stay here. I will leave two more boxes of food where I am parked.

What are the plans of your group?," Lucas said as he set the box of food down.

"I'm not sure we have much of a plan. All of us were in the tunnel cut through the hill when whatever happened, happened. When we came to, we had been thrown around in our cars. There is my Mom, Dad, my younger brother, and me. The other two were in the other car in the tunnel. They are boyfriend and girlfriend or were. I think right now they don't like each other," Larry said as he followed Lucas's action and sat down.

"Hello, second person approaching. Please stop running and raise you right hand in a sign of friendship," Clair's loudspeaker blared.

Lucas stood up and took several steps to his right. He wanted Anna to have clear line of sight.

"Oh, that's my Dad. He was probably worried about me not coming back immediately," Larry said as he walked back to him.

"My name is Harold," Harold said as he came forward.

"I was just trying to find out about your plans. Please stop where you are so we can talk," Lucas said quietly.

"Plans, oh God, plans. I'm not sure I have any plans. Somehow, we have survived this long but we are desperate. We haven't been able to find anything to eat for several days," Harold said as he took Lucas's signal to sit and sat down.

"Harold, let me invite you and your family to join us. Right now, we are on the way to Harrisburg where thirty people are running out of food. I hope to find a few more people like you along the way.

On the way back I will have an empty trailer to carry you back to where we live. There is work, there is a place to build homes and there are supplies to do it with. Are you interested," Lucas slowly explained and ended with his question?

He watched as tears rolled down Harold's cheeks.

"We were coming home from a Christmas family get together. We made the boys go with us against their will. The only reason we are still alive is because the deli delivery truck loaded with meats was in the tunnel with us. From day one I rationed the food.

We went out again and again looking for more. For almost two years we have survived in the tunnel. We managed to close one end up by caving in the hill above it. We are exhausted. We are hungry. We are at the end of our endurance. Are we interested," Harold said his voice breaking as he began to cry?

"Yes, Yes, Yes," he whispered through his tears. Larry was over hugging his father at the end.

Lucas waited a few moments.

"I am pleased I can help. One of the boxes I am leaving behind has a coke for each of you. Please keep the bottles. I am sure we will need them in the future. We will be back in about ten days, and we will be looking for you," Lucas said as he got up and walked back to the SUV.

He left the two boxes and the cokes at the side of road.

"Harold and Larry waved to them as the SUV slowly resumed its journey.

"We will be back. This is Homestead Garden Station wishing you well," Clair announced over her speaker.

"Great job you two," Lucas said as he got back in the SUV and drove off.

Five similar scenes occurred on their way to Harrisburg. Each time Clair monitored the situation and provided the voice that people seemed to listen to.

Each time on his return to the SUV, he thanked Anna and Clair for their support.

He would then recite the number of people that was at a specific location and their names.

After their final stop before reaching the Harrisburg area, Clair declared that the population of the world had just doubled.

Anna countered that if the survival rate was consistent around the world, she would estimate the global population to be between one and fifty million.

Lucas pointed out the wide range of the estimate but that it did not matter since the world originally had more than eight billion people.

Lucas asked Clair to contact the Harrisburg group and have them describe where to meet them.

He was leery about meeting up with such a large group needing food but advanced enough to be broadcasting on the air. Something about the situation really bothered him.

Clara raised the Harrisburg group who instructed them to meet them by the Susquehanna River by the bridge.

Something did not feel right to Lucas. He stopped to look at the map. He pointed at the map where highway Eight five crossed over the Conodoquinet Creek.

He said that he had driven to Harrisburg over the bridge crossing the creek. It was a long and high one. He wondered if the bridge was still in existence.

Here, where Wertzville road comes across 81 will be the place we drop the food. We will go off road just before reaching the location of the bridge and cross the creek and take the back road to that point.

Lucas told Clair to thank Harrisburg for giving them the location and that there would be a few challenging crossings and that she would contact them when they got close.

"Waiting to meet you," was the response.

Lucas stopped the SUV where he was planning to go off the road and cross the creek.

He told Anna and Clair that if he were setting a trap, this would be the location to do it. There was no way across the creek if they went to where the bridge once crossed it. He was going to go on foot and check out the situation.

He took the rifle and his flak jacket and jogged up the road toward the bridge.

Lucas was lying flat below the rise. He had a clear view of the men sitting on the ground by their motorcycles. He counted ten.

The cycles were all black large heavy-duty ones.

Everyone in the group seemed to be armed.

At this range he considered shooting all ten but decided against it. Instead, he crawled back down the slope and jogged back to the SUV.

Anna saw Lucas jogging back at a fairly quick pace.

She looked behind Lucas to make sure no one was following and sighed in relief that she saw no one.

Clair put her small hand on Anna's shoulder and quietly said, me too.

There are ten bikers with a variety of guns waiting for our arrival about a mile up the road. Let's get out of here.

Lucas drove slowly to the creek. He crossed where a shallow rapid crossed over a rock surface. Once on the other side they traveled away from 81 until they reached what Lucas took to be the remains of Wertzville road. He followed this back to where the road crossed Interstate 81.

Lucas found it difficult to relate the map to their specific location. Anna gave her opinion that is did not matter this was as far as they were going to go.

They unloaded the food as rapidly as possible. Lucas had written instructions to plant the seeds he had provided and let them know that this would give the group a late summer, early fall crop.

He also left a note that there would be no more help given to the Harrisburg group. He added that the next time he would shoot the motorcyclists and there would be no warning.

Back tracking on Wertzville road took them away from eight one. They returned to Carlisle where they picked up a group of six. Lucas had opened a vent in the roof of the trailer and had a good supply of water, but it would be a hot ride for those in the trailer.

They were just leaving Carlisle when an inquiry call came in from Harrisburg asking if they were still on the way.

Clair in a steady voice replied we are currently where Wertzville road crosses eight one. We have a flat and are having to off load the trailer to change tires.

We will be there shortly to help you Harrisburg replied.

Sure, you will, Lucas said under his breath.

Clair spotted three dogs crossing in front of them

Lucas honked his horn and the dogs stopped to stare at them. One was a German Sheppard and the other two looked like hunting dogs.

Lucas stopped the SUV and got out and called to the dogs.

The German Sheppard began to wag his tail and approached the SUV. The Sheppard caught the piece of sandwich that Lucas threw to him.

Lucas then called again, and all three dogs came to the back of the trailer. They hesitated for a moment when they saw the people inside but then got in and let the people pet them.

They approached a group of four people that came immediately to the road when Clair called out them.

This group brought three chickens and a rooster with them. They had almost eaten the chickens and only the arrival of the SUV had saved chickens.

Lucas told them to guard the chickens with their lives. They were a ticket to the good life.

They drove well into the night. Lucas kept a close watch in the rear-view mirror, but he saw no pursuit. He suggested they take a short break, let the twenty people that were cramped in the trailer stretch their legs.

He was going to get some sleep.

Anna made it a point to organize the people who had been riding in the trailer. They were all very happy to have been found and to be going to a place where they could work together to survive.

Anna had each of person give their name, age and who they were with.

It was still dark when Lucas a got up. Anna was sitting on a case of canned goods leaning against the back of the SUV. Tramp was at her feet. The three new dogs were laying together by the wheels of the trailer.

The people they had picked up were all asleep in a U-shaped pattern around the trailer.

Anna stood up and gave Lucas a hug. My turn she said as she crawled into the back of the SUV to the spot under where Clair was peacefully sleeping.

The sun had just pierced the grey on the horizon when Lucas got everyone up and ready to ride in the back of the trailer. Everyone had eaten well so there were no complaints.

Lucas checked the map to make sure of their location. They would make it to their last pick up by early afternoon.

Lucas made a point of stopping every couple of hours. This allowed for bathroom breaks and time to just let the body change positions.

Anna got up on the first stop and moved into the front seat. Clair got up at the same time and took up her seat behind Lucas.

They were both back asleep almost immediately once the SUV was once again moving down the highway.

Lucas honked his horn at the people standing by the side of the road.

Larry, his father, his mother, and brother were standing holding hands. The other two must not have made up because they were standing on opposite sides of the family.

Anna suggested that they stop here for the night and continue on in the morning.

Once everyone was out of the trailer. Anna suggested they all have a picnic dinner of sausages, hot dogs, and hamburger. Clair made a point of letting everyone know that everything would come out of a can and there would be no bread.

"But you can eat cake" she said holding up a cup cake in a plastic bag.

Chapter 24: Homestead

Lucas drove slowly up the mountain side. The change in the mountain landscape made the area a foreign land. He realized that the thought was the reality. The soil now had a reddish look versus the sparse but black soil. Even the rather lush yellowish green grass that was growing was a new variety.

The jumble of some Brazilian shopping area loomed ahead and made him think of the train that had been dropped on the mountain side. He had pulled Anna from that wreckage. He looked to Anna sitting in the passenger seat. She was a miracle. After burying more than two hundred bodies he had uncovered as he processed the jumble, he knew Anna had been spared to be with him.

He reached over and rubbed the back of her neck.

Lucas turned up the drive to the homestead. He was tired. He was concerned about the reaction that the Harrisburg group would have. He had twenty-nine people in the trailer that he had to organize into a close working group that had the capability to survive and do the work required to survive.

Lucas stopped the SUV and got out. He stopped to stretch and look around. Everything was as they had left it. Anna and Clair had also gotten out. They were heading straight for the veranda.

Lucas walked around back and opened the trailer doors. There was a cheer from the group and exclamation of wonder as they took in their new surroundings.

Clair was sitting at one of the tables with the dark pine green canvas covered ledger. Anna had already logged everyone in, but she and Lucas decided to verify the information again and to assign work to each person.

Clair had been selected to capture the information. Anna and he would manage the people through this initial step.

Lucas explained to the group that each person would go one at a time and verify the information Anna had. He told them to pick a number from the blue bowl. The number was the order by which they would select a new set of clothes, get a towel, a bar of soap, shampoo, razors, and shaving cream and finally go take a shower. They would each also get a toothbrush and the tooth paste of their choice.

Later, Lucas came out of the house onto the veranda. Everyone, including he, Anna and Clair had showered and cleaned up. The bathrooms had been cleaned.

Anna was supervising a group of five, two men and three women as they prepared an evening meal for thirty. Lucas was pleased when he realized the kitchen was large enough for five cooks.

After dinner, Lucas asked if anyone was interested in a quick walk around the homestead proper. Everyone followed him as he led the tour.

The next morning, Lucas was the one sitting on the veranda with the green ledger. He was handing out work assignments.

He and Anna had made a list of all the tasks that had to get done to incorporate all these people for the long term.

At the top of the list was to get each family or group into their own shelter.

The second was to get enough materials into their hands so they could survive and function on their own.

The final but immediate goal was to give everyone a task that kept everything running in the short term. This was the gardening, animal care, tending to the greenhouse, planning, and preparing for the second priority.

Lucas had the Simon family sitting at the work assignment table. Lucas had no overt racial bias though he might not even recognize the more subtle cultural biases. He was not blind to the behavior of a few of the people they had picked up.

He asked Harold if he would consider taking the job as the lead planner for housing and shelter. He asked Michelle, his wife if she would consider managing and keeping the greenhouse running.

He looked at Larry and Jeff and asked if they wanted to learn how to raise rabbits.

They all immediately agreed.

"Why are you giving us these great jobs," Harold asked?

Lucas could see the emotion in Harold's eyes.

"Because I think you are the right ones for the job," he replied.

Lucas wanted the new world to be fair and color blind. There was no room to waste anyone's talent.

The team of nine he had selected to work the jumble followed him down to the location where the shopping center jumble was located. Lucas began with a walk past the rows of Angels.

When asked why he called them Angels, Lucas replied with a question. Where would you like to reside when it's your time?

The group all talked about the car they wanted when they walked through the area Lucas called the parking lot.

Finally, they approached the jumble. Lucas pointed to the location where he had been putting the light poles and at another that was a pile of twisted metal. The pile of broken glass was at least ten-foot-high and twenty foot in diameter.

The gas station got the most attention.

Lucas explained the work hours. There would be two shifts each day beginning at six am and ending at 6 pm. He explained to the teams how each team would rotate forward one shift each day toward their off-shift day. Everyone would have the weekend away from this work but other work yet to be designated would be done.

Everybody would be expected to be fully trained on every piece of equipment within a month.

Lucas had spent the entire day training the jumble crew. Safety and hygiene were what worried him the most. He used hearing protection, safety glasses, a hard hat, the thin rubber gloves inside of thin leather gloves and steel toe shoes. These were all items he had salvaged from the jumble. He let the team know how dangerous the jumble was and that they would need to be diligent in their safety practices.

He checked all nine members out in the RTV and had each take a loaded trip up to the homestead with a load of food, clothing or building materials.

He made a point of having each person qualify to drive and giving them an ATV driver's certificate. He was surprised at the positive reaction of the group to the certificate.

Next, he demonstrated and had each member operate the forklift. Lucas set up a course through the maze of passages that each member had to drive both forward and backward. In the next few days, each member would do this six times to qualify as a forklift driver.

Finally, he demonstrated the use of the large hoist to be used to pick the pile apart. The driving was similar to the forklift, but the hoist had support legs, a boom and rotation control. Lucas knew this would take most of the team longer to master.

After a brief demonstration he had each of the teams try their hand.

Lucas identified the best three and designated them as the members on the team that would be first to qualify on the hoist.

At the end of the day just before it was time to go up to the homestead for dinner, Lucas called the nine together to organize the three work teams.

He announced the Hoist operator for each team. They were Strong Yu, Asian descent, Bailey Smith, white female, and Martin Parson, African American. He immediately picked up on the reaction of the rest.

He then told each of the remaining team members to put their name on the paper he handed out and write down two of the three teams they wanted to be on.

He collected the papers, led everyone to the ATV, and drove it up to the homestead.

In the evening Lucas, Anna and Clair retreated to the quiet of the workshop. They discussed their day and what they should plan for the following day.

Clair had assumed responsibility for the younger members of the group. She had six in her group. They would focus on sorting and distributing clothes and sorting and storing food goods and managing all the personal care goods.

Anna had assumed responsibility for the gardening, food preparation and spent half her time doing an initial medical examination of each of the thirty.

Lucas had assumed the reclamation from the jumble, shelter planning and the animal husbandry.

Anna had reached a working agreement with Michelle on how to run the greenhouse and garden. She put Michelle in charge of daily operational control. The two would collaborate on the longer-term scheduling of what to grow.

She had reached agreement with Maria Recker that she would run the day-to-day food preparation for everyone on a daily basis and they would work together on the longer-term meal calendar.

Lucas complemented Anna on how quickly she had organized her work.

Clair shared that she had worked with her team, and they had identified six key tasks they would manage. She went on to share the specific tasks.

Both Anna and Lucas volunteered to help her if she needed any help.

"Meeting like this each evening will help me the most," Clair replied.

Lucas complimented her on her leadership skill. Clair was eight, some of her team members where fourteen.

He had followed a similar approach as Anna. Harold Simmon was in charge of getting a shelter plan for the group together. Randy Recker would take over managing the animals. Lucas would focus on getting the reclamation team organized and qualified.

All three agreed that it was time to bring Homestead Garden Station back online.

The next morning everyone was invited to attend the broadcast session.

After everyone was seated, Clair pointed to two white boards where she had printed the words to the song, "We are the world." She let them know they would be featured as the Homestead Singers and made them practice three times.

Then she went on the air.

This is Homestead Garden Station coming on the air with the news, the good news and featuring the Homestead Garden Singers in their rendition of "We are the World."

Puget Sound acknowledged, Africa acknowledged, Germany acknowledged, each station identified the network they were sharing the broadcast with. The only group that was silent was Harrisburg.

Clair began with them. Homestead Garden was pleased to share a substantial amount of food and crop seeds with Harrisburg. We wish them well on their continuing recovery.

The good news is that on the way out we found thirty-two men, women, and children. They are here with me this morning. What a joy for the homestead.

My hope is that all of you are continuing to look for and assimilate all the people of the world.

Now for the Homestead Garden Singers.

Lucas strummed his guitar and Anna led the group in the singing.

The feedback from around the world was a resounding thanks and when would the next broadcast occur.

Lucas took the jumble team down to the site and announced the team make up. He checked to see that everyone was satisfied with the team they were on. Only one person had been placed on their second choice.

Lucas told the teams to spend the rest of the day getting to know each other, talking about how they could work as a team and which team would take first shift on the following day. They could practice the forklift and the ATV, but he wanted them to wait on any practice of running the hoist.

He left to spend time working with Harold for the rest of the day deciding on how to house all the new homestead members.

Lucas asked Clair if she would mind someone building a new home on the Egelston homestead.

Clair's immediate response was that it should be the Simmon's who should live there.

When asked why she thought so, she responded that they were the kind of family that she would have wanted hers to be.

She thought of their home together as her place.

Lucas worked with Harold, who was overjoyed at getting to build on the Egelston homestead. He promised to call it exactly that.

Together they placed the other families into five other locations along the mountain side.

Lucas brought each family in to discuss the location of their new home and to select their house plan. Each home would come with a large work shed and greenhouse.

All the plans were variations of plans, Anna, Clair, and he had made for their home.

Lucas sat quietly as for the sixth time the family sitting across from, he and Harold broke down and cried as they were reviewing the plans for their home.

Harold finally broke the silence by telling them that he and his family had cried as well and that every family had broken down in the same manner.

They all pointed to the fact that their survival finally became real, and they were remembering all the other family members and friends that had not made it.

It was the first time Lucas thought about how it would have felt to have lost his Mother and Father to the event.

He confronted Anna with the question.

Anna replied that she thought about them every day and imagined them doing well in Brazil otherwise I would have to cry every day.

Here I have you and Clair, and I am feeling blessed.

The next day at breakfast Lucas announced the schedule for when a workshop would be built on each of the properties. Everyone would participate in each workshop building session and later everyone would do it again for the raising of the house structures. The entire coming week would be spent getting workshops established at each site.

They would pause other work for one week as all the families moved into the workshops that would serve as home until their houses were built.

Then there would be another week building greenhouses for all the families to go with each workshop.

Again, they would skip a week to allow each family to activate their greenhouses.

Finally, as a group they would raise the frame and cover a house for each of them.

It would be up to each family to finish the interior by engaging the help they needed.

Lucas looked around at the group and was greeted with shouts and clapping.

Each homestead went up as planned. Lucas and Harold augmented the plan and set up a team to go around and help finish each raising event.

Once the homes were erected, they followed up by establishing a finishing crew to help get the interiors finished in a high-quality manner.

The feedback from the families was very positive and both of them knew they had made the right call.

It was after one of the broadcast sessions that Harrisburg finally called. The entire group was still in the broadcast room.

"This is Harrisburg" a new voice came over the speaker. I am Paul Remail, I am representing Harrisburg. We would like to apologize to Homestead Garden for our past behavior. Thank you for the food and the crop seed.

We finally rebelled and kicked out three of our leaders who were strong arming us. They are headed your way in a vindictive mood. Please be careful. They are a mean bunch don't trust anything they say. They were taking everything and literally keeping us prisoners.

There was a long silence that Clair held but then she replied, "We look forward to working with Harrisburg and thank you for the warning."

Clair looked over to Anna and Lucas to see if she had handled the situation properly.

"Good response, Anna and I will take it from here. Everyone please go about your daily schedule," Lucas announced.

Harold had followed him and Anna into the workshop. Harold looked at the two and said he was going into the house for a cup of coffee.

Lucas let Anna know that he would be gone for most of the day on an errand.

Please don't take any chances," Anna said as she watched Lucas take the high-powered rifle and a 357 from the armory.

He put on his bullet proof vest and hiked down the driveway to the jumble. Martin and his team were working that morning.

He suggested they go talk to Harold about helping to finish one of the homesteads. He stopped there for the ATV. He gassed it up, put the supplies he wanted in the back and left.

Martin looked at Angie and Rick, his other two team members and commented that he would not want to be any of the guys coming down 81 and began his walk up the road to the homestead.

Lucas drove the ATV northward on 81 until he came to the long downhill slope where he planned to make his stand. He put the ATV in sight and placed a mat down beside it.

He had no intentions of trying to talk to any of the three.

He was struggling with his decision to kill all three. He could not take a change of letting them go up to Homestead.

About an hour later Lucas heard the roar of the bikes and finally saw the dust tail they were kicking up behind them.

Lucas stood up as the bikes reached the bottom of the long hill.

He was surprised by the action of the lead cyclist who began firing at him.

Lucas got down on his mat, sighted in and slowly pulled the trigger. The bike continued its approach up the hill and Lucas thought he had missed.

He responded to the other two shooters in the same methodical manner and in his peripheral vision watched the first two cycles crash as he placed his last shot.

Lucas stood up and looked down the hill. The last biker had gotten within one hundred feet.

He walked to each biker and fired the 357 with a shot to their forehead.

He returned to the ATV. He rolled up his mat. Took the shovel and dug a shallow grave on the side of the road. He loaded each of the bikes onto the ATV.

On his way back he put the three large cycles in the parking lot next to the smaller ones.

He then drove slowly up to the workshop.

Harold looked up and asked if there were any more Angels. He remembered the first day he had seen Lucas and had almost attacked him. Clair had warned Lucas. Harold had looked up to see Anna with the rifle sighted on him. Harold knew he had almost become an Angel on that day.

Lucas looked at him and said there were three more Angels, but they would stand at the devils gate for their reward.

Harold understood. He also recognized the fundamental strength of both Lucas and Anna. Both were gentle and both could be deadly.

Lucas walked through the garden examining each of the plants. The irrigation channels were doing their job. The garden was calming. It quieted his nerves.

Anna approached him and asked how he was feeling and if they were safe.

Lucas stopped and looked at her. In his previous life he would never have taken the action that he had on this day.

He replied that they were safe, and he was feeling well. Seeing Anna made him surer that his actions were the right thing to do.

She handed Lucas his favorite spam sandwich and went over to the rock by the spring and sat down.

He came over and said they should set the guiding social structure for the group. They needed to agree on how the group would function. The action of the Harrisburg three and his response highlighted the need for establishing a governing structure.

Anna leaned over and kissed him. She thanked him and quietly told him his new child thanked him.

Lucas slowly processed the words as a smile spread across his face. "Does Clair know,," He asked?

Anna replied that she planned to tell her after dinner that evening.

Dinner went by slowly. Anna waited until Jeffery and Samuel, two single young men that did not yet have a home and were living in the barn left the table.

Ok, what did I do wrong today Clair spoke up after the two left?

Oh, it's not what you did but what Lucas and I have done. You will soon have a new baby brother or sister.

Clair jumped up and kept shouting "O my gosh" as she rushed around the table to give Anna a hug.

Clair knew she had her good news story for the following day.

Chapter 25: Muri, John traveling Africa

*M*uri looked up to the cargo ship laying on its side. It towered at least a hundred feet above him. John and he were alive because this ship and its dead crew had been dropped from the sky almost on top of the now missing village where he and John had lived.

He and John knew they would never see their parents or any of the villagers again. The fact that they stood together looking up at hundreds of cargo containers was a miracle.

They had spent the last few months building their multi-story encampment from containers. It featured a fully equipped natural gas cooking area with an exhaust hood located in the center of a twenty-five-meter diameter center courtyard. There were two bathing facilities on each side. They had an osmosis-based water filter system supplying the drinking and cooking water. Their current living area was in the container located opposite of the entry gates.

The two of them felt that their new living facilities bordered on being extravagant.

Muri was going down the check list he and John had developed in preparation for their search for other survivors. Gasoline and water created the biggest load. They had chosen to carry dried noodles and canned tuna as the main food.   It was both easy to manage and it was what they had the most of.

Muri and John planned to go to the Indian Ocean and return. They would then go to the Mediterranean and return. Then they would go to the tip of Africa. Their final trip would be to the Atlantic.

John complained that they would be old men by the time they completed their journeys.

"Let's hope we become old men with beautiful wives and many children," Muri replied.

Muri asked John if he had something more important to do with his life.

He was acutely aware of how alone and isolated John, and he had become.

They had not gotten any response to their radio transmissions. Either their radio was not functioning or no one else was on the air.

Muri looked over to John in his dark maroon colored leather out fit with a matching helmet. He complemented John on his stylish look.

John replied that Muri looked a lot like the character in the star wars movie and that perhaps they should get him a cape to wear.

Each of their helmets had a small built-in radio allowing them to talk to each other as they traveled. This would really help in making it a closely coordinated trip.

They planned to make Pweto their first stop.

When they arrived at the location where the ferry used to operate, they stopped and stripped down to their shorts.

Muri walked as far upstream as he could and waded in. He swam across carrying only a pair of flip flops. John followed close behind.

They then walked toward the area where Pweto had been located.

There was nothing to see. Muri commented that it was as if God had swept the area clean.

Muri was turning to leave when he saw movement from the corner of his eye. When he turned to look, he saw nothing. He walked toward the location he thought he had seen the motion. John was some distance away already heading back toward the river. He signaled to John to follow him.

He and John stopped and looked down at the emaciated figures where they lay on the ground. They were nothing but bones, bulging eyes and a rib cages. There were three of them. They all still had a pulse and were alive. Just barely alive.

Muri and John carried all three to the river's edge.

Muri swam across and returned with water and three cans of chicken soup. It was hard to tell how old any of them were, but it was clear they were not adults.

Muri shared his father's story about starving people being given food too quickly and dying because their system were not ready for it.

John and he warmed some of the chicken soup and gave each of the three about a quarter cup of the broth.

They then followed the soup with about a half a cup of water.

Muri made several more trips across the river as he brought over the materials to make a comfortable camp.

John claimed the night watch and told Muri to get a good night sleep.

John looked up wishing he could see the moon, but the sky was still covered by a thick cloud cover.

Muri woke up early in the morning to find John still tending to the three. He had not awakened him for the mid watch.

Muri thanked John for a good night sleep. He informed John that he was going to return to the compound and bring back a ferry.

Muri swam back across the river. He returned to the compound where he left the food and gas laden wagon. He then went to the ship and got one of the large life rafts the ship carried.

He gathered several hundred feet of line and ten long metal poles. The final tool was a heavy sledge to be used to drive the poles into the ground.

Muri returned to the river with his load. He found a deep crack in the rock along the riverbank and drove the two metal stakes down into it. He bolted on a ring and secured the heavy line to the ring. He then tied a light thin line to the end of the heavy rope.

He inflated the life raft and pulled it as far up stream as possible and guided the life raft across the river.

John helped him pull the raft up onto the riverbank.

Muri carried the sledge and two metal stakes up along the bank until he was opposite the stakes on the other side. He again found a crack in the rock and sank two stakes with the sledge.

He then pulled the thin light line through the ring attached to the two stakes.

Muri asked John to help. He watched as the light line went taunt and then the heavy five-centimeter manila line approached the edge of the river.

He and John were leaning at almost a forty-five-degree angle pulling with all their might as the river tried to pull the line downstream.

Finally, John wrapped the lighter rope around his waist as Muri ran up and guided the larger rope through the ring.

He and John both fell on their butts as the large rope cleared the water and the power of the river water ceased trying to pull the rope from them.

They sat and laughed as they took a minute to recover.

Muri helped to pull the heavy line as tight as they could and then he tied it to the ring. He and John then pulled the raft up to the rope that came across.

Muri slipped two pulleys onto the main line and tied a line from each to heavy duty lift rings on the top side of raft.

The final step was to take the small line back across to the other side and secure it at that end. The light line severed as the pull line and the heavy line held the load against the pull of the river.

John looked at the final product. It had taken most of the day to get everything set up.

He asked Muri when he had learned to make the ferry.

Muri replied that this was exactly how the old ferry worked. He shared that he had been fascinated how it was set up and figured out how it worked. He never thought it would be something he would need.

John updated Muri on their patients. The young lady that had signaled them had come around. She had opened her eyes. Said thank you and then closed her eyes.

John had immediately checked her pulse to make sure she hadn't died. She was OK.

The other two, are taking the broth, seem to be doing OK as well.

Muri and John looked at three and decided that they could all be taken across on a single trip.

He and John gathered all their belonging and put it into the raft.

Then carried the three and put them on the raft.

Muri sat in the front of the raft and John in the back. Together they pulled the raft across.

They loaded everything on the wagons and in what seemed no time they were approaching the compound gates.

Muri had left one gate open, and they were able to pull into the center of the compound.

They left the three on the wagons.

They chose to make the container in what they called the ten o-clock position the hospital recovery room. The shower and facility room was at the nine o-clock position. Muri pointed out that this would make it easier to get the three cleaned up as part of the recovery process.

Once their "hospital" was set up and arranged so the three could be put into proper beds. John and Muri carried them in.

They agreed that on the following day they would give the three a proper bath, and make sure they are physically OK.

John pointed out that after that it would be just a matter of time to get their bodies functioning properly.

He and John were both exhausted.

Muri opened a can of salmon and offered it to John.

He then suggested they both get a good night sleep.

The next morning John made the observation that the container wall was coated with frost. Both he and Muri rubbed their hand across the container surface.

Neither had experience this before.

Muri made the observation that the sun was not warming the earth as before. They might face a major cold spell the way it happened during the Ice Age.

John pointed out that the Ice age had massive glaciers that covered the north and south, but they were in Africa.

Muri gave hunch of his shoulders. We also have never had an ocean-going vessel in Pweto. He pointed out that there were several containers with vacuum packed foam that they could use to insulate the walls of the containers.

John learned that the name of the young lady was Angela. She was the same age as he and Muri. The two boys with her were Mugabe and Joseph and were friends similar to Muri and John but three years younger.

Their families had been on an outdoor outing together. The two had run ahead to be the first to the back of the large overhang. As they reached the back of the overhand, they were suddenly thrown up into the ceiling and when they recovered, they were alone in a strange and alien world.

They had wandered about looking for anyone. They ran into Angela. Angela had been out with her boyfriend. He had gone out to get some gear from his backpack when she was thrown up into the roof of the tunnel they were in. Later, when she regained consciousness, she ventured out looking for her boyfriend.

She had run into the two.

They had stayed together and periodically found something to eat.

Muri and John found them at their last moments before dying.

Muri looked at Angela and asked if she was strong enough to take care of the two boys. It was time he and John proceeded on their journey.

Muri was instructing, the three foundlings as he thought of them. He pointed out that there was an abundance of food.

He showed all three how to use the radio transmitter.

He had set up the radio frequency to the one that was of the helmet system and set up a small transmitter on one of the wagons. This would allow he and John to talk to each other and to Angela.

He made sure the three staying behind knew how everything in the compound functioned.

He was nervous about leaving them alone at the compound.

Angela put her hand on his shoulder and told him that she was quite capable of keeping the compound in good shape.

John looked at Muri and simply said, oh one in black, it is time we left, and he walked out to his bike and wagons.

John and Muri returned to the river. They spent a day ferrying all their equipment across. This allowed them to take the more direct route to the coast. It was a route with a greater number of towns as well.

Once across they got everything loaded and proceeded on the journey.

John using a bull horn periodically called out. The population of the area had always been sparse. Now it was empty of not only people but of all the animals as well.

Muri stopped and pointed to an object laying in the road. It looked like a dog.

He approached it slowly and cautiously. The dog did not move. It appeared dead.

John walked over to see if it was dead. The dog opened its eyes.

John opened his bottle of water and dribbled it on the dog's tongue.

Muri left John as he went to investigate the noise coming from one of the few bushes in the area.

There he found three white and black spotted puppies that had just been born and were seeking something to eat.

Muri arranged a space in the wagon where they could put the mother and her puppies.

We have chicken broth but no dog food. The mother will have to eat what we eat until we get back. There is plenty of dog food on the ship.

Angela reported that pigeons had landed on the center canopy. I think they are looking for food.

"I am going to feed them our scraps. I can't wait for you to get back with the puppies," Angela reported over the radio.

Muri was pleased to have found the dog and her puppies. The pigeons finding the compound was also a good sign.

Muri commented that John and he were good finders. Three people and three dogs. He verbally pondered which would be most useful in the long run.

He got a trio raspberry over the air.

<u>Chapter 26: Cualli, Tosi, Sailing East</u>

𝒯osi was looking across the water at the island that was still a great distant away. She was happy to see the two dolphins speeding along side, playing in the waves. They had sailed all day away from the atoll where they had washed up. The atoll that had saved their lives.

Cualli looked to the island that had doubled in size but still seemed to be a fair distance. He commented that it would really help to have a map with which to navigate.

Seeing the white sand strip trimming the water's edge confirmed their arrival to their first target. What they had thought to be the top of a mountain was instead a large ship sitting in the middle of a large atoll.

Both Cualli and Tosi began laughing at the same time as they saw was on the shore.

They were sailing past the main building of the Grand Vegas Hotel and there was a beach cabana down on the beach. It was impossible!

Cualli and Tosi had slept on the beach in front of the hotel just this past summer. This was on the beach of Puerto Vallarta. They did not have enough money to even rent a hotel let alone stay at one of the top hotels on the beach. They had slept in their sleeping bags in front of the hotel and listened to the Mariachi group playing on the lawn.

The hotel security had run them off the next morning. That was the best spring break that they had enjoyed together.

Now both of them were looking at what would seem to be an impossible sight.

How could it be Cualli mumbled as he continued to sail around the island?

He guided the cat through a narrow opening into the interior of the atoll.

The site of the hotel had been shocking. The huge cruise liner looming a hundred feet above them appearing as it was anchored in port miniaturized them to the point of insignificance.

Cualli approached a large modern sailing sloop looking as if it was purposely anchored but realized that it was just floating on the loose. He hailed the sloop thinking that there would be someone on board.

There was no response, so he brought the cat in parallel to it and he and Tosi tied the cat to the sloop.

Their catamaran was about six meters long. The sloop seemed to be at least three times longer.

Tosi's first impulse was to jump on board. Then she stopped and let Cualli go first. He was better at handling the sight of dead bodies than she was. She was constantly waking up to the memory of the site of the many dead bodies they had buried.

Cualli did a quick search and called out an all clear.

The sloop clearly was one of the boats in the luxury class. It had a forward bedroom that was finished with an almost white wooden floor. The furniture, closets and trim were a dark red cherry wood. The king size bed was covered with a red trimmed cream-colored bed spread. The room looked as if it had just been cleaned.

Tosi ran forward and jumped onto the bed, gave a big sigh, and kept whispering that this must be heaven.

Cualli wandered into the kitchen area. He ran his hands along the black marble countertop past a gas stove top with a microwave mounted above it and exhaust vents above the stove and below the microwave.

He reached the end of the counter where cherry wood cabinets were mounted. He opened one of the doors and caught a cup as it fell out.

He walked past the stair set on the port side. One set went down the other up and out to the aft deck. The bar counter was the same marble as the rest of the counters. Cualli picked up the four chairs meant to be at the bar. Two were wedged into the built-in black marble topped six-person booth, one was behind the bar and the other in the middle of the room.

He had planned to investigate the contents of the bar but there was a large amount of broken glass.

Cualli then took the starboard steps down to a door that opened into a bedroom with four bunk beds, two on each side of the room. A closet to the back of the room and a chest to the front of the room.

He went to the port side and looked into the other bedroom. It had a queen size bed the same back closet and front chest. This room had a sitting area with a large dark brown leather reclining easy chair.

Cualli took the port stairs up and out to the back deck.

He walked to the wheel. He turned and looked the length of the sloop and up to the top of the mast.

Tosi joined him and they just stood quietly looking around the lagoon. The sloop was in an almost perfect condition. The engine compartment looked undamaged, and the engine appeared functional. The main inner deck area had some broken glass on the deck and the cabinets all needed to have some broken items removed and straightened out.

The battery of the sloop was dead. Cualli looked around the engine compartment and saw a gas-powered electric generator. He checked it out and pulled the starting cord. On his third pull the generator came on.

He laughed; his Dad's lawn mower never started on the third pull.

The lights on the sloop all came to life.

He could hear Tosi giving a cheer.

He checked to verify that the battery was charging, and then he went up on deck.

He got a big hug from Tosi as he exited the engine compartment.

He quickly checked to ensure that the lights were off and then sat down at the table in the kitchen area.

He watched as Tosi tried the stove, the microwave, and the faucet.

She turned to him with a big smile and said that she was going to take a shower and get a good night sleep.

The next morning, they took the sloop's dingy and rowed to the giant cruise ship. The gang way still attached to the middle of the ship was hanging down from an open door.

Cualli was able to reach the bottom of the gangway and pull himself up the gang way. He looked around and found an emergency ladder that he unrolled and lowered down to Tosi.

Cualli was on the hunt for a battery, some global navigation maps and any kind of food that was still edible.

He suggested they start on the bridge to see if they could find a layout of the ship.

Cualli noticed the ship had a slight tilt toward the port. He guessed it was sitting on the bottom of the lagoon. He chose to take the exterior ladders up to the bridge in hopes of avoiding any bodies.

They saw no bodies on the decks they passed and none in the bridge area.

Cualli went straight to the center map table with the drawers full of maps below them.

Cualli collected all the maps that featured the Pacific and rolled them up. He was going to study them to see if he could figure out where he and Tosi might be.

He then found the diagrams of the ship's interior.

He located three cafeterias, six coffee shops and a shopping hall. He also located several mechanical workshops, and the engine room.

Tosi suggested they go shopping for food first and the battery second.

Cualli pointed to the radio transmitter. He said he would be back to see if he could get it working.

This time Tosi with the ship's interior lay out in her hands led the way to the shopping deck.

The twenty-foot-wide hallway, lined with shops on both sides was littered with a wide variety of merchandise, broken glass but no bodies. Tosi commented that the Event happened close to midnight. That meant the stores would have been closed. She checked one of the shop doors and the door was locked.

Tosi and Cualli stepped in through the window of a convenience store. She filled her bag with M&M's, some candy bars and carefully opened up the refrigerator and retrieved two orange sodas.

There next stop was one of the many restaurants. They were surprised that it was as neat as they found it. The freezers were no longer cold and the food stuff inside was spoiled. It did not smell as bad as Cualli had expected.

Tosi found the dry good storage rooms. Each had some degree of disorder but in general it would be easy to straighten out. There were many bags of rice, beans, lentils, flour.

They agreed that they would no longer have to worry about having enough to eat.

The sprouting potatoes and the limp but still edible carrots were the big surprise. Planting them would be a priority.

They took some rice, beans, and a canned ham to take back to their sloop.

Cualli and Tosi spent the next few days getting organized. The first thing they did was to plant the potatoes and carrots. They did not want to miss their chance on missing a future crop.

Tosi inventoried and catalogued the location of the food they found. It would take them many more weeks to go through the entire ship.

They stopped after the second day when they thought they had at least a one-year supply of food that they had moved to the yacht.

They found two bodies in the crew's living quarters.

Cualli designated a location on the atoll as the cemetery and buried them. Tosi said a prayer over them. They looked at each other and walked arm in arm back to the dingy.

Cualli investigated the communication arrangement on the ship and learned that there were two complete systems. They were modular which made it easy to take one of the two apart and transport it to the sloop.

He mounted the radio on a shelf behind the table. It had taken all his courage and energy to hoist himself to the top of the mast to mount the antenna.

The sloop was named Vanity. They disliked the current name. Finally, they agreed on the name; *"Pacific Event Survivor."*

They spent a day removing the old name and painting on the new name in gold script.

This was followed by smashing a bottle of Champaign across the bow and officially launching the sloop with its new name.

Tosi put their radio system on the air, "This is Pacific Event Survivor coming on the air. Please respond."

She did this on seven separate frequencies. Cualli sipped on his coffee and nibbled on his warm muffin. He looked at Tosi, raised an eyebrow, and lifted his shoulders in a signal of disappointment.

Then a clear voice broke the silence as it responded.

"Pacific Event Survivor, this is Puget Sound, pleased to hear you. I have six other stations on my network.

How many are you?"

Tosi was beaming as she responded that they were only two.

How many are you?

Tosi's face lost much of its color when she heard the reply that Puget Sound was only six. Puget Sound also replied their network was only about two hundred people.

She looked at Cualli. Puget Sound was connected to six other stations, and they could count only two hundred people. What had happened to all the people?

Cualli looked up from the map in front of him and pointed to some islands on the map.

He then told Tosi to imagine their flight up into the air with the Earth spinning and passing by below them. If their path had been directly west and nothing else occurred, then they would have landed where they did.

He emphasized the point by thumping his index finger on the place they were currently located. The only way for us to land where we did was for the Earth's mantle to rotate under us.

The Earth is eighty percent water, which is why there are so few people.

Chapter 27: Recovery and the Norfolk

Lucas was on the air talking to Puget Sound, the global network, and the broadcast room full of people.

"It is time for us to begin to address how we the survivors will work together to build the future of the world."

Sixty-eight people of all ages, backgrounds and ethnicity sat before him. Clair was the youngest and Mathew Glazer a Harrisburg survivor was sixty-six.

"You saved us all," Mathew commented and got a chorus of agreement.

He had survived because he was in a drainpipe recovering from a drinking binge when the Event occurred. He was now a changed man and focused on helping everyone recover.

Lucas looked at Mathew and thanked him. He made the point that this was not about gratitude but about getting organized to create a future in which the human race could recover, flourish, and create a culture of learning, acceptance, and respect for all individuals.

Lucas had discussed his vision in detail with Anna. He proposed modernizing the US constitution and implement a form of government similar to the one the US had established.

Anna had distributed some documents for everyone to read. She had paper copies for those in the room and she had transmitted them to all stations.

We are the people and the only ones that can re-establish a government for us the people. There are few of us. This is the opportunity to create a global unity. The US constitution can serve as a historical reference. We can create and agree to a new constitution that fits the current situation.

In the next few days, we will create this new constitution and all of us will have the opportunity to sign it. Imagine your name on the Global Constitution.

"This is Puget Sound. We have read the initial materials you sent out. We have shared it with all stations connected to us.

Everyone is looking forward to the next several days as we work through our new constitution. Everyone on our network is excited."

Lucas looked at the people in the room and could feel the positive energy.

He signed off the air and let Anna take over the meeting.

The meeting started on Monday and by Wednesday, everyone was put on a team. This included those who were on the air.

On Wednesday they were interrupted by a faint voice announcing that Pweto Station was on the air and would like to participate.

Clair took over the communication and asked the network to see if they could get a better connection. It was Pacific Event Survivors that provide a signal boosting retransmission that linked to Puget Sound that made the communication feasible.

There was new energy in the room and in the meeting as another five people joined in establishing a new world order.

The meeting continued throughout the week and representatives from each group met on Friday to finalize the document. There was one hundred percent agreement and alignment to the new "United World Constitution."

It embraced the three chambers, the Supreme Court, the Senate, and the House. Representation was granted based on location and population. One Senator for each location, one Representative for each five persons. There would only be three Supreme Court judges at the beginning. Each position was limited to six years and each person could only server for two consecutive terms. They could serve again after sitting out for two terms, but they could be in one of the other chambers.

Lucas was the first to sign, Anna and Clair followed and then everyone in the room added their signatures. Everyone on the global network gave their name, clearly spelled it and Anna added them to the original master document.

Clair was nominated and became one of three judges on the Supreme Court. Harold spoke up saying he would be honored to serve on the court and was voted in unanimously. And in a surprised Mathew Glazer from Harrisburg was nominated by his group and claimed the third supreme court seat.

Anna was elected Senator representing Homestead Garden. They would also elect five Representatives.

Puget Sound was granted one Senator and two Representatives. Pacific Event Survivors was granted one Senator and one Representative.   Pweto Station was granted one Senator and one Representative.

Agreement was reached that if more survivors were found, the area where they were found would automatically have their representation adjusted.

When it came time to select the President and Vice President. One name was put forward for each. Lucas was uncontested as the nominee for president and elected unanimously. A surprise nomination came in from Pweto. They nominated Muri Lamand. This led to a long discussion but since no other nominee was put forward, Muri was elected the first Vice President.

"This is Puget Sound and the noise you hear is the celebration of our journey into the future in this new Globally United World. We are honored to be part of the future. Thank you," Lucas.

Similar messages came from each of the other stations.

The celebration went on the rest of the weekend and a formal dinner was prepared for everyone at Garden Homestead Station.

Anna was making the observation to Lucas that their new Supreme Court had a twelve-year-old girl, a black former shoe clerk and a recovering alcoholic as Supreme Court judges. The three had met and Clair was selected as Chief Justice.

Lucas chuckled and added that they at least had the sense to elect the smartest of the three to lead them. He was not so sure about the rest of the survivors who had selected him as the President.

Clair was just signing off the air when a new call came in.

Garden Station this the USS Norfolk.

A cheer went up from the roughly dozen people who had participated in the latest program.

Clair had left the transmit button on and had broadcast the cheer.

As you can hear we are very pleased to hear your call. How can we help you?

Clair was at her professional best. No one listening would have guessed she had just turned twelve and become the Supreme Court Chief Justice.

Lucas knew that her voice and manner projected an image of confidence, control, power, and maturity.

This is Commander Daniel Mosely. We were going to ask you the same question? Since you asked first, we would like to meet with you to decide what to do next. We have traveled from port to port for more than two years.

You are the first survivors we have connected with. We are short on food. How do you fare?

We would be pleased to resupply you. You have returned just in time to celebrate with us. President Mayfield has just been elected and sworn in by the Chief Justice two days ago. He happens to be on location. Give me a moment and I will put him in touch with you.

Clair stopped transmitting and began to count.

Lucas looked at her and asked what she was doing.

I am going to get the President. Do you think people expect to find him standing by the radio transmitter?

I am putting you in position of authority over the Armed Forces as per the Constitution Clair replied in a serious voice.

Commander Mosely, I was able to get the President and pull him away from a meeting. Here he is.

Commander let me introduce myself and let's not be too formal. I am Lucas Mayfield. Everyone here is very pleased that you and your men have survived. You are the only military unit to have checked back in.

We have the food supplies you need. Are you able to dock or bring your boat to where we can transfer supplies to you?

It is good to know that the country is reorganizing. So far you are the first signs of life we have made contact with. We are currently almost to where I 95 once crossed the river.

We will bring you a first round of food resupply. Do you have a full complement? Lucas asked. If they did it would be more than one hundred people.

The reply affirmed a full complement.

How quickly should we plan on getting re-supplied, Commander Mosely asked. He did not want to sound desperate, but his men had not eaten in two days.

"We will come in two waves. We will bring enough food for two or three days then we will need your help to move the additional supplies," Lucas replied.

"Thank you, I look forward to our meeting. This is the USS Norfolk signing off."

"Well, we may yet make it through our mountain side roadblock that hinders our descent toward the sea. And we will proceed to mine the new find young Larry and his friend found in the valley below the train wreck. In the direction I guess now is officially East," Lucas said as he organized the relief team that would resupply the Norfolk.

Almost a week later, Commander Mosely and about half his crew had made the trip back to Homestead Garden.

They were all sitting at the dinner table set up in the grand shed. The dinner had been prepared with the help of all the people of Homestead.

The meal consisting of slices of ham, rice with black beans and a fresh lettuce and tomato salad was simple but very tasty and filling.

"I want to thank you for the outpouring of support you have shown. I need to get re-oriented. I am not sure what my actions should be. The military side of me says I should be in charge. My personal side is not sure," Commander Mosely said as he ate the last of his tasty pork.

"Let's make it official. I would like you to be the Chief of Naval Operations and for the foreseeable future I would like you to also fill in as the Chairman of the Joint Chiefs of Staff. Your consul on the matters pertaining to the defense and the protection of the nation and the continuing search for survivors will be valued by your President," Lucas said solemnly and then beamed a smile.

He looked over at Clair and winked at her in acknowledgement of her previous comment.

"Thank you, Mr. President. I humbly accept this position. I believe this satisfies my need for inclusion and participation. What are my first duties," Commander Mosely inquired?

Anna led the response, "First, I believe you should meet all the members of the Government that is present here; the Chief Justices, two of which are present; the members of the Senate, three which are present; the members of the House of Representatives, ten which are present. Later you should travel to Harrisburg to meet with the rest. You will be key in connecting the west coast to the east coast and to travel around the world so that the Vice President, who resides somewhere in Africa can make a trip here.

"Let me introduce those who are here."

"Let me get this straight; one Supreme Court Justice is only twelve, one Senator is fifteen and two members of congress are fourteen and seventeen. What happened to age limits," Commander Mosely exclaimed!

I am Harold Simmon, honored to have been selected as a Supreme Court Judge. We selected the smartest of us to be the Chief Justice. She is our voice on the air, she has the wisdom most of us take a lifetime to acquire.

In this new world, intelligence, not age is a key criteria. The act of stepping up and contributing, getting the job done and doing your best by everyone around you is the reason your crew was resupplied, and you ate so well this evening.

Commander Mosely apologized immediately. Please understand how isolated my crew has been for the last two years. We will contribute our share and we will support your efforts in uniting the world.

"Here is to all of us working together, He raised his drink in a salute to the table.

Chapter 28: West to East, North to South

Finding the mother dog and three pups gave Muri hope that they would find some people.

He asked John how the mother and pups were doing.

They proceeded slowly along the shore of Lake Mweru toward Puta.

They were averaging about fifteen miles per hour.

John replied that they were all doing fine. He commented on the barren nature of the countryside.

He then got on his bull horn.

"This is Rescue Mission Alpha calling out to any survivors. Can we help you?"

Muri asked about the mission alpha lingo.

"Oh, I figure it's our first mission. The next trip it will be Rescue Mission Bravo," John answered.

Muri joked that he would start calling him professor.

A few hours later as Muri turned away from the lake at Mununga, John's announcement drew a small group.

Muri observed that it seemed the young were the survivors.

"John, let me go to the group with some food and then we can decide what to do with them," Muri said.

John and he were both armed and had discussed what to do in case they were attacked.

There were seven in this group, and all appeared young. Muri approached and passed out some water. He asked if there were any others and learned the seven were the only ones.

He then handed each a can of soup and a small can opener. He asked how they had survived.

One of the seven introduced himself as Alex. He explained they had just arrived from Puta. They were looking for food.

Alex explained that the seven had been playing in the cities old well. The well had some old side tunnels where they often hid and played. They had almost drowned when the well water floated up.

The well was capped by a cement cap and when the water hit the cap it burst through. We were all pinned against the top of the side tunnel. When we fell to the floor a huge amount of water fell back into the well, but it was salty. We climbed out to find the town gone.

Muri asked how they had survived. Alex said they caught the fish in the well. The returning water was filled with many fish, and they were able to dive with a spear and catch them.

Muri signaled to John to come forward with the food. They unloaded enough food and water to last the seven at least ten days.

He instructed them to go to the edge of the lake and to use that water to bathe and stay healthy. John pulled out a tarp for them to use as a shelter.

Muri left the mother dog and her puppies with them as well. He made a point of making sure that everyone knew that one puppy was designated for Angela.

"Oh, thank you for the puppy. I can't wait until you get back," Angela said when Muri told her.

Muri and John left the seven at the edge of the lake and proceeded on to Luwinga.

Along the way they found a cat, a goat, and a monkey.

John commented that they were becoming a small zoo. The monkey seemed partial to Muri and wanted to ride on his shoulder.

They approached a group made up of nine people. There were two three member families, and two boys and one girl. They were all traveling together.

Muri and John provided them with food and instructed them to continue to the lake to join the six they had left there.

They left all the animals with them and proceeded on toward the east.

John commented that they had gone a third of the way and already more than tripled the population of the Pweto compound.

Let's hope we have that problem and more," Muri replied.

"Well, you wished for the problem, and we have it," John said as he smiled at Muri.

They arrived to where T2 crossed the border into Tanzania and became A104 at what had been the city of Tunduma. Now there was nothing.

They continued on and found a camp of twenty-two people that had come together as they traveled. The camp was desperate for food. John and Muri gave them most of the provisions they had brought with them.

Muri instructed this group to follow the tracks of the motor bikes back toward Pweto. He let them know that he and John would return to take them back to a new home.

Angela volunteered to come out and guide the groups back to the compound.

Muri and John both said no, they wanted to be present when they brought everyone to the compound. They wanted to make sure they did not lose control of their camp.

That afternoon, Angela called back excitedly that she had made contact with several broadcast stations. There was a global meeting going to organize the recovery.

The effort was being led by a group called Homestead Garden Station, there were also survivors in Puget Sound and one in the Pacific another in Europe. She had agreed to participate in getting a government set up. She had volunteered Pweto to be part of getting the world organized.

Muri and John listened as Angela read the proposed constitution. They were impressed with the proposal. They made a couple of comments and suggestions. Angela was directly participating over the radio with a group calling themselves the Pacific Event Survivors. This group was relaying the signal on to a group in Puget Sound who in turn connected with Homestead Garden.

Muri and John continued their journey even as they participated in the effort through Angela.

Muri was shocked when Angela informed him that she had nominated him to be Vice President. He was more shocked when she called him back and let him know that he had been unanimously elected to the position.

John bowed before him and commented that he had never been in the presence of a Global Vice President before.

The next day they made twice the distance they had been making. They found one person. Ocaba was an old maintenance technician at the Mbeya Maternity Hospital. He survived because he had been underground in a maintenance tunnel working on the sewer line.

They gave him food and a tent and told him they would be back in a few days.

"I will be sitting right here on the road. There is no were else for me to stay," Ocaba replied.

They stopped at Irringa where 104 joined A7. At their current rate they were within a day of their destination.

The next day, as they made their way along A7 through the Mikumi National Park, they came upon what was a huge area strewn with the remains of what appeared to be a shopping center.

"What can this possibly be," John asked as they approached the jumble.

"It looks like the remains of a city," Muri replied as he slowly walked toward the edge of the jumble and stopped to scan across it.

"This will be very valuable to us. There is a little of everything," John said.

Muri suggested they continue to their final destination of Dar es Salaam and on the return, they should see if they could find food to take back with them.

As they approached their last destination, Muri almost hit a frantic young woman who ran out and fell in front of his motorcycle.

Muri and John helped her up. She just kept repeating, "Don't leave me," as she cried in John's arms.

She finally responded to Muri's question of what is your name?

Kerin, Kerin, Kerin is my name. Please don't leave me.

John handed her a bottle of water and reassured her that she was rescued. John gave her a can of tuna that she gobbled up, putting almost all of it in her mouth and rolling her eyes. It was clear she had not eaten for some long period of time.

Please don't leave me. There is nothing here. No one. Kerin again repeated.

John took her to the cart behind his bike and had Kerin sit down.

Muri recognized the hysteria and sympathized with her.

He called into Angela and let her know that he and John had made it to the coast and were starting their journey back. He told her that they were returning with fifty-nine people.

He instructed her to ask Homestead Garden and President Mayfield for twelve more representatives.

Angela let out a cheer and said that she and her two friends were clearing the containers and preparing the living quarters for the returning foundlings.

Muri thanked her and said he would be sending her information on who to put where, as they made the trip back.

Muri envisioned the container encampment. There were eleven containers on the ground level and six on the second level. Another eight containers could easily be added on the second level.

John and he had already designated one container as the hospital room. Another two containers were the bathroom and shower facilities.

Across the courtyard was the kitchen container. The cooking area was in the center of the courtyard. He and John had taken up residence in the container directly across from the entrance gate.

He and John decided that the single males and single women would be housed in the containers immediately to the left and right of the entry containers.

They put the families on the second floor.

They let Angela know the arrangement. She and the other two were to do what they could but Muri expected each arriving person to help in getting the compound fully functional.

As they returned, once again Muri looked at the jumble of what had been a shopping area from some city somewhere in the world. How it ended up in the middle of one of Africa's largest nature preserves was a mystery.

This time he and John were making it a priority to comb through it quickly to find any food that they could use to feed the people they were escorting back to the compound.

Kerin was riding behind John. She had settled down and fallen asleep as they bumped roughly back along the road.

She woke up when they stopped. She seemed to have recovered from the hysteria she had exhibited when they had found her.

Kerin was asked to stay with the motorcycles and wagons. Muir and John agreed to take separate paths into the pile before them.

Muri went slowly through the maze. The stench of decomposing bodies made him feel a little nauseous.

Muri stopped when he came upon some large wheels of cheese. He was surrounded by a variety of cheeses. They were about dinner plate in diameter and a little thicker than the common brick. This he recognized as a treasure!

He looked around for a way to carry as many at one time as possible. He located a moving dolly and stacked ten cheeses on top of each other and went back to the wagons.

He made six trips in all and was just loading his last cheese into the food wagon when John returned with a surprise.

John was carrying several cages toward the wagons. He had two cats, a dog, five rabbits and a plastic bag full of fish.

He enrolled Muri and Kerin to return with him to the pet shop he had found. They gathered up some more birds and any other creature that they could find.

Muri, John, and Kerin loaded up all the animals and much of the pet food they found in the shop.

Muri then led the way back to the cheese shop. There, they gathered all the smaller cheeses and a variety of sausages.

Three of the four wagons were loaded with food. It was time to guide the people they had found back to the compound.

Later Muri would describe their return trip as one of leapfrog logistics. He and John would pick up a group and take them to the edge of the Lake. They would then return to those the farthest behind and take them to the Lake. They did this three times

Once to the lake everyone was instructed to follow the shore toward the location of the ferry.

John and he took the last group all the way to the ferry.

He and John brought all fifty-nine new members to the ferry by the end of the day.

He had everyone set up camp. He and John had decided to process the new people and get their information before taking them into the Pweto Compound.

Chapter 29: Cualli, Tosi, Australia

"You say you know why we are so few," Tosi repeated what Cualli had just said as a question?

"Yes, I know why we are so few," Cualli said with certainty.

"The Earth is eighty percent water. So, eighty percent of what went up in the air ended up in the water. We went up in the air and took air and water up with us, but we passed out due to lack of air. We were lucky not to have suffocated. I think most people died while in the air. The rest died when they landed in the water or if they landed on the land they were battered and broken. We experienced a miracle. We landed in the water and were able to get to land," Cualli expounded.

"But why does the sun rise in the west," Tosi asked again.

"The sun is constant. What has changed is the orientation of the Earth. Its iron core remained stable and rotating as it has always done. The mantle, much like the skin on a basketball, rotated 180 degrees and changed rotation direction in harmony with the rotation of the core," Cualli explained.

He carefully and neatly put a W where the E had been on the map's compass rose.

This time when they went out of the lagoon Cualli knew where he was heading, and he found the Islands he located on the map.

Cualli and Tosi were two hundred miles west of French Polynesia in an area of about twenty atoll islands. They planned on a quick pass around all the islands and then a run to the main French Polynesia Island of Tahiti.

"I hope we find a few people. It would be nice to have a couple so we could at least play cards at night," Tosi said as they approached the next atoll.

They visited sixteen of the atolls in succession. They circled those where the entrance to the center was inaccessible or the interior waters too shallow for their boat. They found no one. Even palm trees were missing on most of them. Many of them had been reduced to their stone structures. The sand was just beginning to wash in and built the atolls up once again.

"It is amazing how different these atolls are from what is on the map," Tosi said with disappointment as they left the last atoll behind.

They were sailing on to the main island of French Polynesia. Their hopes of finding anyone had been greatly reduced.

"This is Pacific Event Survivor. Sad news today: We have finished sailing the atolls that are within one hundred and fifty miles of our base lagoon. We have found no one. We are now sailing east. In about a day we will arrive in the French Polynesian Islands. We are arriving at Tahiti. Wish us luck in our search," Tosi broadcast.

"This is Puget Sound; thank you for the update; very sorry to hear the sad news. Good luck in your search. I will share this with Homestead Garden Station.

The New World Constitution has been approved. President Mayfield has been sworn in. Pacific Survivors have one Senate Seat and One House of Representative seat. Mweru Station has also been awarded the same number. Muri Lamand of Mweru Station has been elected Vice president.

"Pacific Radio, this Mweru Station Africa, thank you for the relay. We are so excited about our inclusion and look forward to working with everyone on our global recovery. Muri and John have found some survivors." Angela excitedly broad cast after hearing the news.

Angela immediately shared the news about his election to VP with Muri. She had previously not said anything about putting his name up for Vice President.

The news about the world getting organized and communicating with each other helped Tosi and Cualli over their disappointment at finding no survivors.

They looked at each other. Tosi came over to where Cualli was standing behind the wheel and gave him a hug.

They had each other.

Tosi was at the helm the next day when the mountains of the Island of Tahiti came into view.

"These islands are very different from the atolls we have visited. Here the volcanoes thrust their cones high into the sky. The slopes come down to the sea," Cualli said as he took the sloop as close to shore as he dared.

He had a detailed map of the area, but it was based on conditions before the Event. Now he was finding the maps had some errors. He was also cautious about any new obstacles that might have been dropped from the sky.

They had agreed on a plan that took them counterclockwise around the island.

Tosi was using a bull horn to call to shore.

The journey began at the narrow part of the figure eight part of the Island. The wind was cooperating, and they were sailing smoothly as close to shore as Cualli dared. He was able to stay within hailing distance until they reached the point at Tautira where he went out beyond the reefs.

Once around the island and to the other side he found his way back in closer to shore at Teahupoo. Once again, he crowded as close to shore as possible. And though the map showed a village or city, they saw nothing from the boat.

"Hello the shore. Please signal if you hear this call," Tosi said for the hundredth time.

They were making their way into the waist of the figure eight shape of the island opposite from their starting point when Cualli thought he saw motion on the far beach.

He pointed to the nine o-clock position of the port.

He took the sloop back around for another pass.

Both he and Tosi were excited.

The sloop was a pleasure to sail. It handled the maneuver smoothly as they circled back on the location.

"There, on the shore, what is that" Cualli said pointing?

Tosi had the binocular out scanning the shoreline.

"I'm sorry but that is a scrap piece of plastic caught on a piece of driftwood fluttering in the wind," Tosi said in a disappointed voice.

She too had gotten excited and was now let down.

Cualli and Tosi continued along the shoreline for the rest of the afternoon.

At Punaauia they came back in close to shore.

They almost missed the group running along the beach waving.

Just by chance Tosi happened to look back.

"Stop, go back, there are people on the shore. We almost missed them. Swing back around. Swing around," Tosi said excitedly as she hit Cualli on the shoulder.

"Fire your flare so they know we saw them," Cualli said excitedly.

In the excitement he almost turned the sloop the wrong way. He managed to calm down and focus on bringing the sloop around and back down the beach.

About halfway along the beach was a freshwater runoff. It was filled with water as far back as Tosi could see. The group had made their camp along its banks. It appeared there were about twenty people. Most of them were men.

Cualli brought *The Event Survivor* in and set anchor at the mouth of the runoff. This seemed a good spot to spend the night.

"Let's be careful. We want to help but we do not want to be victimized. They look hungry. Let's take an ample supply of food and water. I think for now the canned ham and beans will be all," Cualli said as they loaded the skiff.

He also had his pistol in the boat.

"We will handle this with diplomacy," Tosi said as she watched Cualli put the gun in the boat.

Several of the men came out and helped pull the skiff up on the shore.

They were greeted with an excited group all speaking French.

Tosi replied in Spanish. That didn't work very well. She then spoke English.

"Yes, I understand you very well," one of the women replied back in an English that was a mix of Australian and proper Queen's English.

Cualli commented quietly to Tosi that the speaker sounded exotic. He noted she was also very good looking and was rewarded with an elbow in the ribs by Tosi.

"I am Tosi, this is Cualli. We have brought you food and drink. Where do you live? What are your needs," Tosi said as she stepped out of the skiff and began to distribute the food stuff?

"I am Cammi. We are trying to find enough materials to build a place to stay but it is as if the island was swept clean. Even the airfield is gone. Thank you for the food. We are very hungry," Cammi replied.

"Why don't we take a break while you eat? Then we can talk about how to proceed. We can offer you all food, and a place to live," Tosi shared.

Tosi sat in the sand by Cammi while Cualli stood by the beached skiff. He was still wary and wanted to stay close to skiff and the pistol he had put in the bow.

The six women were mostly office workers. Two were married but their husbands were not among the survivors. The other four including Cammi were single.

The fourteen men ranged from nineteen to fifty-four years of age. They were all cobalt miners. All twenty had survived because the office had been built into part of the mine itself. The miners had been down doing their mining. One of the women was a doctor who had been down inspecting conditions in the mine.

"Let me invite the women to sleep on the boat tonight. Tomorrow we can take everyone onboard and sail back to the atoll where we have plenty of living space on a grounded cruise ship," Tosi offered after everyone had eaten.

Cammi shared this offer in French to the rest of the group and received nods of agreement and smiles on all faces.

"In the morning we will feed everyone a large breakfast on the sloop and then get under way," she continued.

It took two trips out to the sloop to get the women onboard.

Tosi toured the women and they decided how to share the two back bedrooms. The rooms were designed to sleep four each. With only five women each had a bed of their own.

The focus for the evening was the shower. All the towels were utilized as the six lined up to take their first shower in weeks.

"Well, you certainly made yourself popular by offering the women the use of the shower," Cualli said with a smile as he sipped on a cup of hot coffee.

"Oh, that felt so wonderful. Thank you so much for inviting us on board this evening," Cammi said as Tosi gave her a cup of coffee. Soon the table was surrounded by exuberant talk.

The doctor, Neva, spoke some English and they were soon talking about what to do when they got back to the cruise ship.

The men came on board the next morning and ate breakfast in shifts. They took in the luxury of the yacht. Soon most were dosing on deck enjoying a smooth ride as Cualli sailed around the Island and back to the atoll.

"There is plenty of work back at the atoll to keep everyone occupied. We still need to continue our search for others. If we get the cruise ship off the bottom so it can level itself out, it will be the perfect home for all the people, we might find. We need someone to plan and to guide the group otherwise nothing will get done," Cualli speculated to Tosi.

"I believe Cammi, Neva who is the oldest among us and a doctor and I can organize the group. You could go out in search with several of the men. Everyone could be put to work to leverage their capability in the area of their interest. We can ask for technical guidance from our world network when we need it," Tosi volunteered.

"And we can ask for three additional representatives to sit in Congress," she concluded with a smile.

Chapter 30: Epilogue

ℒucas, his hair now grey gave Anna, the angel, who had dropped from the sky, a hug as the waves washed over their feet. They were out on a walk along the beach of Cancun. Clair's two daughters were chasing their cousin who in turn was causing the gulls to rise into the air to get out of the way.

Homestead Gardens was a treasured memory now buried under ten feet of snow. The long winters and cool seasons continued. The world was going through a major climate adjustment.

The Event survivors were a lucky few.

The world population just cleared four hundred thousand.

The seat of the world government was now in Veracruz. Representatives from around the world came once a year to conduct face to face business. The rest of the year business was conducted on the radio internet.

Constant communication and sharing of learning and of actual resources allowed the survivors from around the world to join and maintain a single world government. It was a government focused on ensuring the survival of everyone in a manner that let everyone participate.

Lucas had pushed for it from the beginning. Muriuki Lamand "Muri" and he had been elected twice as President and Vice President. Muri's friend John Mustafa and Tosi Lopez, a Pacific Event Survivor, were just finishing their second six-year term.

The United Support Force (USF) is still under the command of Admiral Daniel Mosely. He claims that his only love are the ships and the people under his command. His fleet of the nuclear submarine Norfolk, a light destroyer, twelve newly developed sailing hydrofoils and two large transport freighters provide the support required around the world.

They were all converted to sailing vessels.

This force took food, materials, tools, and workers to the places needing it, when they needed it.

Lucas and Anna's son, Noah, was developing the air wing for the United Support Force. Noah was constantly talking about the new aircraft being developed based on gliders and on lighter than air blimps.

The farms leaned heavily on greenhouses similar to the ones Lucas established at the homestead site. Every household had a family greenhouse. Many also raised chickens for their eggs.

The surface of the world suffered a total reorientation of materials that was still a challenge to deal with. The beaches required cleaning every morning to remove the debris that washed up. Plastic material reduced to small chunks was recovered by passing sand through screens.

Bodies and body parts were now rare, but mass graves covered thousands of acres.

In every survival area, the survivors were dealing with the dramatic change. The soil, stones everything was different. Some rivers ceased to exist. And the climate was different and erratic.

There were still many functional satellites orbiting the earth. A group of the survivors were working on establishing communications with them. This was a challenge due to the security programs installed to prevent hacking.

Lucas was confident within a couple of years the global communication would once again utilize many of these satellites.

The younger generation was re-establishing development in the computer technology.

Each area had some young survivors engaged in its reemergence.

Lucas had confidence in their ability to win the day.

He was struck by the irony that somewhere waiting to be found and entered were facilities that have stored the DNA of many of the Earth's animal species and the seeds of almost all plants. No one knew where these facilities might be.

A group of survivors existed with the sole purpose to find these underground, safe and unfortunately very well-hidden facilities.

The US facility though bomb proof had been built above ground. It was not where it was built. It was now probably underwater in the North Pacific.

Minimal sea trade had begun. Africa had four major seaports. Australia one, the Americas have three.

Lucas was still amazed at how few ships had survived. Light boats were abundant, and he could go water skiing, but freighters were few. Recreational use of gasoline was not allowed so he also could not water ski or us a power boat for recreation.

Sailboats were sought out and cherished.

Ship building was going to take a long time to recover. There were no steel mills, a fair amount of fiber glass and the resin used to make boats was being recovered. This was being used to recondition and commission more sailboats.

The broadcast news seemed like a throwback to the old days when everyone would gather around to listen to the radio farm report. The news highlights now were "grape vine roots discovered," "Coffee tree yields first crop," "Pineapple plant yields fruit," "First Jasmine tea leaves picked," "Chickens and Rooster proud parents."

Lucas found it interesting how much he enjoyed these news items and how popular the features were with everyone.

Lucas encouraged everyone to stay focused on achieving long term survival status. New life, new accomplishments were important to a population that was living off the remnants of a destroyed population.

Survival capabilities needed to be established before they ran out of the wealth of the previous world.

Most provincial biases were discarded. Color, gender, and age were not points of discrimination rather they were most often points of pride.

Lucas had pushed for and gotten free basic health care, free education through college, minimal daily sustenance for everyone written into the constitution.

Everyone was required to produce. People worked for their pride. They worked for life. They worked to re-establish life on Earth.

Lucas was now the leading breeder of rabbits, skunks, ground hogs and just about any other animal sent his way.

He worked with a group breeding the fox, wolf, badger, and a pair of bears.

Every animal received help when discovered. Cattle were very few and no longer used for food.

Meat in general was seldom on any table.

The list of available fruits, vegetables, rice, potatoes, and beans was long and growing longer. The greenhouses all competed in the variety they produced.

The Event was devastating. The recovery continued to be challenging. The Survivors were kinder, less judgmental, more focused on helping each other.

Competition in sports events was coming back to the forefront. Soccer, baseball, and basketball were the primary global sports.

Lucas looked out at the slowly setting sun.

He held the love of his life at his side and looked at the pinkish grey clouds light up as the pale Sun's edge met the water.

The grandkids held up a small crab.

This was his paradise. It was more than he had ever imagined would be possible when he woke up in the cave after the Event.

The End.

About the Author

Ronald E. Mueller
remwriter95@gmail.com

Ron has a fascination with the scientific thought process. He writes stories just beyond the possible but clearly achievable with just the right technological breakthrough. Ron's science fiction almost seems true. His heroes are not superhuman but rather the regular guy put into a must do situation.

These must do characters are of all genders and races. The bad guys are equally diverse.

Ron's background as a control system engineer and production system optimization has exposed him to how equipment is made. He is a professional engineer and has been around most of the developing technology of the day.

Ron was born in Brazil, grew up in Iowa, served in Vietnam, graduated from the University of South Florida, worked for Procter and Gamble for thirty-seven years and has been happily married for forty-three years.

He is the father of three great offspring and now the grandfather of three really smart grandchildren.

<u>Characters in the story</u>

Name		Role
Lucus	Mayfield	Main Character (US)
Anna	Zepf	Main female character (Brazil)
Clair	Egelston	young girl that survives
Amanda		Lucus's first love
Rachel		Amand's friend
Jim	Egelston	Neighbor, Clair's father
Evelyn	Egelston	Neighbor, Clair's Mother
Jeff	Baker	Survivor Washington
Ellen	Dexter	Survivor Washington
James	Mercer	Older couple on the ship
Judy	Mercer	Older couple on the ship
Lara	Alves	Young Newly married couple on the ship
Thiego	Alves	Young Newly married couple on the ship
Muriuki	Lamand	Pweto Africa Survivor
John	Mustafa	Muri's best friend
Larry	Simmon	US survivors
Jeff	Simmon	US survivors
Harold	Simmon	US survivors
Michelle	Simmon	US survivors
Maria	Recker	US survivors
Randy	Recker	US survivors
Mary	Recker	US survivors
George	Recker	US survivors
Samuel	Miller	US survivors
Randy	Johnson	US survivors
Rick	Sanders	US survivors
Angie	Dix	US survivors
Bailey	Smith	US survivors
Rachel	Sams	US survivors
Martin	Parsons	US survivors
Strong	Yu	US survivors
Angela		rescued by Muri and John
Mugabe		rescued by Muri and John
Joseph		rescued by Muri and John
Ocaba		Old Maintenance man found by Muri

Tosi	Lopez	Survivor Pacific
Cualli	Cordova	Survivor Pacific
Cammi	Girard	Survivor Pacific
Neva	Fournier	Survivor Pacific

Published by: Around the World Publishing LLC.

www.ingramcontent.com/pod-product-compliance
Lightning Source LLC
Chambersburg PA
CBHW060235100726
47907CB00003B/643